MW01199297

Rachel H. Kester

AMISH CROSSROADS SERIES

Box Set 2: Books 5-8

Copyright 2015 © Rachel H. Kester

All right reserved

This is a work of fiction. Names, characters, businesses, places, events and incidents are either the products of the author's imagination or used in a fictitious manner. Any resemblance to actual persons, living or dead, or actual events is purely coincidental.

Amish Crossroads Series

A note for our readers...

You are going to read 4 episodes of the series Amish Crossroads: books 5 to 8.

If you enjoy these books, make sure to sign up here:

http://www.amishromanceseries.com/amish-crossroad/

for information about next releases, discount offers and FREE book from Rachel H. Kester and other great Amish Romance Series authors.

It's completely free, and never miss all the best in the incredible world of the Amish Romance Series.

Lastly, you will find in this book some uncommon words in italics, they are not English, but Amish. We will send to you a list with the translation of all the main Amish words as soon as you will be register to:

http://www.amishromanceseries.com/amish-crossroad/

We look forward to reading with you ;-)
Sincerely Yours.

Rachel H. Kester

Table of Contents

Rachel H. Kester

Amish Crossroads Series

Rachel H. Kester

BOOK 5

Chapter 1

I stand here watching my husband work tirelessly to put up another house and if I were to be honest, I was starting to feel a little homesick. I'd only heard from my *dochtah* a couple of times. I could hear how much she missed me in the tone of her voice. Jacob is feeling that he has a sense of accomplishment and a purpose in his life. I'm not saying that I'm not feeling the same way. I do feel that kind of hope every time that I look into one of these kids eyes. It's that hope that we cultivate, so that they can live for another day.

"You kids have always been there for me and I know that you get a lot out of these talks. I'm glad, because I do too." I loved these kids like they were my own. I feel like we are connected like mother and *dochtah* or even son. My *shtamm* is my life and revolves around Jacob and my *dochtah*. "I just want you know, even if I'm not around, somebody will be. That's a promise that I intend to keep."

"Does this mean that you're thinking about leaving?" I could see that this little kid named Michael had grown accustomed to having me around. "Please don't go." It felt like he was tugging at my sleeve. My heart was breaking. I really didn't know how to answer him.

"I know that a lot of you are thinking the same thing that Michael is. I understand that you'll miss me, but I do have a family of my own. I don't think that I'll be gone long, but I need time to reconnect. You go home to your *maemm and daett* or the person that cares for you every day. I am without that. I have enjoyed our time together. Let me put it into terms that you'll understand. You all have a favorite toy that if you were without it for a significant amount of time….you'd miss it." I saw all of them looking at each other.

My long dress was fanned out behind me and it was a little hot for something of this attire, but this was what I was used to. Jacob was smiling at me from over near the house and he was pounding in a nail and wiping his brow with the sleeve of his shirt. It was hard schaffe, but we were accustomed to rolling up our sleeves.

"I guess I can understand. I would miss hammer. He has been with me through all of this. I would never want to be without him." I could see what he was talking about. He was holding onto this GI Joe doll with a death grip. He had nicknamed it hammer and my husband is infinite wisdom had decided to help him. He had made him a small tiny hammer that would fit perfectly in that action heroes hand.

I closed the Bible and we all bowed our head in silent prayer. It was the way that I had always ended these little sessions. I felt more connected to the children that I did with the adults. I guess they just had a different way of looking at things. They were more childlike and innocent. I loved that.

They dispersed and went to play. I went over to Jacob and tapped him on the shoulder. He turned around and his face lit up like the 4th of July. He hugged me and then he relinquished his hold. He looked me in the eyes and I think he knew instinctively what I was thinking.

"Bethany, I can see that something is weighing heavily on your mind. If I were to hazard a guess, I would say that it was your *dochtah*. I know that you've been missing her and it's written across your face. I wish that I could take away that pain."

"I would like to go home. I know that that might sound selfish, but it's the way I feel. I want us to talk to the Deacon and find out if we can leave as soon as possible. I need to recharge, hold my *dochtah* in my arms. It's the only way I'll know that there is a light at the end of the tunnel."

I could see his sweat sticking to his skin. The *brau* shirt that he was wearing was almost translucent. "I didn't want to tell you, but I was feeling the same way. It's just that I haven't seen my *shtamm* in a long time. It feels like forever. I know that it hasn't been, but it feels like that. I think that we should go and talk to the Deacon. I know that replacements are on their way, but we weren't supposed to leave, until the last bus. We can make a plea and hopefully he will see that we have been just going through the motions." I could never love anybody more deeply than I did with Jacob. It was never ending. It was like his heart was a part of my own.

Hand in hand, we went over to the Deacon and we told him how we were feeling. He listened without judgment and didn't say anything, until we were finished.

"You both have been *schaffing* tirelessly and I appreciate all your efforts. There's no reason why you can't go on the first wave. I'll make the arrangements. It's just that we are going to miss you. I just hope that you will want to come back after seeing the devastation." He was obviously gauging us to find out if we were still as committed to this cause. I could probably speak for Jacob and say that we were.

"We don't think you have anything to worry about, Deacon. Jacob and I are on the right path. We know that. Trust that we will be back. We give you our solemn vow on that." The one thing that we could pride ourselves on was that we were worthy of our word. It was after all our bond to each other and to anybody else that would come across our path.

Chapter 2

We had begun packing and I felt this momentary heavyweight coming down on my chest. I was holding the last piece of clothing that I had to put into my luggage. It felt like a chapter of my life was ending. I knew that it wasn't and that it was just a momentary reprieve, until we returned. I felt this presence behind me. Jacob was standing there and he put his hands around my waist from behind.

"I know and I've made some great friends here. We made a real difference, Bethany and I hope that you know it. I don't think I could've done this without you. I feel like this is a real steppingstone for us. Maybe when we return home, our *shtamm* will finally understand that we had to do this. I know my *daett* didn't like this and thought I was just going through a phase. I need to face him and tell him that I've found my calling. I'm ready to do that now. You gave me that courage, Bethany and that is something that I will never forget." The gentle feel of him against me was more than enough to raise my spirits.

"Jacob, I don't know why, but I feel like I'm abandoning them and I know that we've made a difference. It just feels like we could do a whole lot more, but we are only two people. That's where our replacements come in. They will pick up where we left off." I picked up my bonnet, putting it on over my head and I walked out with luggage in tow.

We both stopped short, completely stunned and speechless. In front of us was the entire delegation, plus many of the locals that had come out to bid us a fond farewell. I know that they meant well, but I suddenly found myself welling up in tears. I knew that I needed to see my *dochtah*, but this was my surrogate *shtamm*.

The Deacon stepped forward "I didn't ask them and they volunteered to see you off. I'm sorry, but with a close knit community like this one things like this don't stay a secret for long. You really made people think that there was a way out of this continuous hell. They see that you've come here on your own volition and you've done remarkable *schaffe*. They wanted to at least give you fond wishes and hope for a speedy return." I felt like what we've been doing was worth something.

People were truly appreciative of what we did. I don't think I could've gotten anything like that from any other profession. I really didn't even consider this a profession. It was what I was supposed to do with my life.

Thinking of my *dochtah*, I began to wonder what kind of path she would take. Would I be ready to let her go? I suppose everybody has that feeling about their own *bobli* and to me she would always be my *bobli*. It wouldn't matter how old she got.

"I really appreciate you coming out to see us off. You really didn't have to." Before I could say anything more, people were coming about to give us small gifts of their gratitude. A local farmer had cultivated a week's supply of vegetables to give to us for our journey. I really didn't know how to tell him that we probably couldn't take it with us. It would be a hassle at customs. He looked, so happy that it didn't seem right to take away the joy that he got by giving it to us.

"I want you to have this. That way, I'll know that you are coming back." Little Michael came forward with his action figure and I knew that it was his prized one called hammer. "I want him to protect you and then you can bring him back when you return." It was such a selfless thing to do and it made me kneel down and touch his head in a gentle and soothing manner.

We heard the bus coming and it was loud. I didn't realize it was going to be that loud. It was coming right up to us and the few of us that were leaving on this day. The door opened and the driver, an African American with experience in his eyes smiled. He came out to greet us. We had seen him a couple of times during our stay here.

"I don't know if I can take this, but I will borrow it and have it back to you before you know it, Michael." I didn't want to take it away from him, but he looked so downtrodden that I didn't see any harm in keeping it as a reminder of what I was missing.

The driver said "I'm going to put your luggage inside and then we should get going before you miss your flight." Everybody gave us kisses and hugs. We returned them in kind.

We stepped up onto the bus together after the other dozen people that were going home had already taken their seats. The door closed and we all stayed by the windows to wave, as the children chased us the entire way.

"We'll be back; Bethany and I think you know that deep down into your heart. This place still needs us and the rebuilding that we have done has only scratched the surface. Those new replacements are going to need training in building. I'm going to have to come back. Then again, you are just as proficient with a hammer as I am. We'll both teach them together. It's what we did when we were here, and I don't see any reason why that has to change." I looked back and I was able to watch as the dust swirled around us. Finally, it obscured our vision from those that were running on the side of the road.

He put his hand in mine and I looked up to him and then we kissed lightly. I then settled back with a sigh of relief.

Chapter 3

It felt a little different to be relaxing. We didn't have a hammer in our hands. We didn't have people looking to us for guidance. It was almost like we were on vacation. It's something that we both deserved. So, why was it that I was feeling like something was wrong. We were going home and I was going to see my *dochtah*. What could possibly go wrong with something like that?

"Bethany, I can see that something is bothering you. You're not going to be able to rest, until you tell me all about it. I know that this is hard, but you and I both decided as a couple that we wanted to take a break from all of this. We've given them hope. We've given them some place to lay their heads and that is just the start of what we're going to do for them. We've even gotten them involved in the Bible. Kids that don't really know any religion have suddenly found their faith."

"Jacob, I know all that and I feel like we've really done something here. It's just that something is nagging at the back of my consciousness. I don't know what it is, but it's a sense of foreboding. It might be just because of those black clouds in the sky, but I don't think so. I'm not saying that I'm having a premonition or anything like that. I'm just saying that I feel like maybe we should stop and go back." I knew how foolish that sounded, but I couldn't help feeling like there was something bad over the horizon.

"My mother used to have these feelings when I was growing up. She called them women's intuition and I've learned not to ignore. She was the one that knew that my *daett* had had some kind of serious accident. I guess underneath it all, all women have this unique insight. I just think that this might have something to do with the fact that we are leaving. This could be your guilt manifesting itself into something that isn't there."

I jabbed him on the arm playfully "I didn't know that you had a license in psychology. Did I miss something, or did you go to school to study the human mind?"

"It's not anybody else's mind that I know. It's yours. I know how much this hurts you and give you a certain delight at the same time. It can't be easy to reconcile those two things. Is it possible that you are letting these two things conflict and become hard to justify in your mind?"

"Jacob, I suppose it's possible and not going to say that it isn't." I lay back against his arm, feeling safe and not safe. It was a weird sensation and then I heard the brakes on the bus slide against the dirt road. It jolted us out of our seats. We all craned our necks to see what was going on. From our vantage point at the back of the bus, we really couldn't see anything, except that driver had stopped all momentum.

There were mumbles of loud voices and even Jacob began to show concern on his face. He was taller than me, so he might have seen something that I didn't. "Bethany, I need you to stay here." Like that was really going to happen. I think he knew that from the way that I was looking at him with defiance in my eyes.

"My name is Mitchell and I am the one that is in control here. The sooner that you get that through your thick skulls, the sooner everybody will get out of this alive." I saw him standing at the front of the bus with a makeshift mask that was made from a handkerchief. He looked like a modern day bandit with all black clothes, except for the denim shirt that he wore with the first two buttons undone. I could see this chain and I was almost certain that a cross was attached to it. "If anybody does exactly what we say, then nobody gets injured. Trust me; we will hurt you if we have to."

I could see the look on Jacob's face. I was trying to stop him, but it was like trying to put a leash around an elephant.

"What exactly is it that you want. This is a delegation of peace and we are volunteers on our way back to our home in the States. What possible reason could you have for stopping this bus and putting everybody's lives in jeopardy?"

"Isn't it obvious? This is all about money and we intend to have you reach out to your families. Then you are to tell them that you need $10,000. Once the money is received, then we will gladly let you go on your way. In the meantime, we are commandeering this bus. We can't afford to have the authorities or anything that they call the authorities these days getting wind of this. Trust us; it's in your best interest to pay attention." Mitchell couldn't be more than 18 years old. He was a rebel with a cause. I could understand his mentality to help, but this was not the way to go about it.

"I really don't think you understand. We are volunteers and our families don't really have that much to call their own. We're an Amish community. We live a relatively minimalist lifestyle. We only have what we need and not what we want. There's no technology, except for some propane stoves. We don't even own a laptop, computer or any kind of television." This didn't seem like something that Mitchell wanted to hear, but he had already started this ill advised course of action and it didn't look like he was going to back down in front of his own people. I didn't want to voice it, but I knew now that my feeling or woman's intuition was right on the mark.

Chapter 4

"Bethany, I don't think we have anything to worry about. They are obviously amateurs and kids at that. They are under the mistaken impression that we are rich. They should have done their research, but they are acting on instinct alone. They want to do something to help their people. Instead of waiting for us to get to them, they have decided to come to us in a more dramatic way." Jacob was right and Mitchell was obviously running on pure adrenaline alone. His people were looking for him for guidance and those that he had gotten to help him with the ransoming off hostages were now looking at each other slightly nervous and confused.

"Excuse me, Mitchell." He heard his name and he turned around. The bus was bumping along a very jagged path that wasn't meant for any type of vehicle. "I hate to tell you your business, but your people seem a little jittery. Maybe a pep talk from their leader would go a long way. They need to know that you have everything under control.

Again, I don't want to tell you your business, but I don't want anybody to get hurt because one of your people has decided to take matters into their own hands." I didn't even know if Mitchell was his real name. For some reason I didn't think that he had lied about that.

He listened to what I had to say, but I wasn't sure he was really paying any attention. He finally stood up and addressed everybody on the bus. "We just want you to know that we're not doing this because we are bad people. We're doing this because we want to help those that we care about most get back up on their feet after the devastation that you've seen with your own eyes. If everybody cooperates and there are no would-be heroes amongst you, then we shouldn't have any problems."

"Mitchell, I don't understand why we had to take this bus. They obviously don't have any money. We searched their belongings and found nothing that was very useful. The clothing and food will go a long way. What we need most of all is money and we haven't seen a dime between any of them."

"Carl, I really don't think this is the place or time to question my decisions. If you have something to say to me, then I would rather you do it in private. I've already told you all that I would get you what you wanted. We're not asking for much from either one of them. $10,000 is a mere pittance to most of these people." He was trying his best to rally the troops, but I could see dissension.

"I really don't think that you thought this through. We don't have anything of value and all you'll be doing is worrying our family's needlessly. Maybe it's time that you look within yourself and to the word of God. He is obviously with you and you hold him close to your heart." He immediately touched the cross through his shirt. He most likely didn't even know that he was doing it.

"I don't know what gives you the right to preach to me. I don't need to hear you talk and the only thing I need from you is for you to reach out to your families. They will obviously want your safe return and would do anything to get it. The most predictable thing in this world is a family's love for their children. If we have to, we'll make an example out of one of you, just to show that we are serious about what we're doing here today. Just so you know, we do appreciate everything that you've done, but that still is not enough."

"My wife is right and you really are barking up the wrong tree. This is an Amish outreach program, a humanitarian aid effort that is meant for good will. There's nobody here that has a rich *shtamm*."

"What the hell is a *shtamm*? I think that you should shut the hell up and sit down. I didn't ask for your opinion and if I wanted you to say something, I would pull your chain." He had turned his gun on Jacob, placing it against his temple. You'd think that anybody in his shoes would be shaking, but Jacob was different. He stood there with his eyes wide open and focused. He wouldn't say anything and he sat back down, but he did show no fear in front of overwhelming odds.

The green leather of the seat on the bus was sticking to our skin and even though we had the windows open, it was almost too much to take.

I could see this sense of relief coming over the faces of those that were now holding the guns. It obviously meant that we were almost to our destination. They were happy to return home as heroes. They couldn't be considered that, until they got the money. They most likely would hide us somewhere out of sight and out of mind. That way nobody would get suspicious and they could work behind the scenes without any interruptions.

As we drove through what this constituted as a road, I felt like my kidneys were going to come out of my chest. I had no idea how the bus was even able to withstand this kind of punishment. You could hear the squeaking of the shocks, as it took the brunt of the attack of all the rocks and ruts in the road.

"You two are obviously the leaders. You can speak for everybody else. That could only mean that they look up to you. If you really want this to be over, then I would suggest that you convince them to play ball. My people have itchy trigger fingers. I would suggest that you tell your friends here that any kind of hope for escape will never come. The only way out of this is to give us what we want. It's really a no brainer. Once this is over our people will classify us, as modern day robin hoods." At the sound of that, his people let out a roar of approval.

They raised their guns in the air in a sign of solidarity with Mitchell. "As for your idea of getting in touch with my Bible. I really don't know what to say. God has forsaken this land. I don't have the kind of faith that I used to. I don't even know how you could, after seeing what has been done to this place." He was obviously hurting and I could see the solemn nods of all those that followed him.

Their backs were turned and they were talking amongst themselves. We could've easily slipped out the back door and we looked at each other and began to contemplate our own escape.

Chapter 5

I think we both knew that we weren't going to do anything about it. It just wasn't in our DNA to leave our friends to fend for themselves. We counted in our heads to twenty. In all that time, neither one of them had looked in our direction. It was too bad that we weren't those kinds of people. We could've easily gotten off this bus and they wouldn't be the wiser.

"I know what you are thinking."

"I know what you're thinking too, Jacob. Let's forget that we had even the notion of doing anything like that. It makes me feel guilty just thinking about it." Mitchell and his people were talking in hushed tones and they really weren't paying attention to anybody. I could see that a couple of my friends were deciding to make a stand. We had to put a stop to this. If we didn't, then there most certainly would've been bloodshed.

I saw Timothy about to stand up. I put my hand on his shoulder and shook my head vehemently. He looked towards Jacob for a second opinion and got the same stern expression in return. He finally settled down. Apparently, others had seen what was going on. They were now contemplating the same thing, but realizing that we might have had a better way.

"Jacob, we're really going to have to find some way out of this. They are relying on us. We need to show them that we're not just going to lie back and take this. I don't condone violence. I'm sure that we can find some reasonable solution that can be taken with words instead of actions.

"I still think that you might've been on the right track, Bethany. He has a strong moral fiber. It's just that his faith has been tested as of late. He can't be blamed for that. He really should have thought about a more constructive way to bring his people together. This is only going to alienate a lot of them. I don't even want to imagine what they'll do when they find out that he really can't deliver what he promised. We need to force him to see this was wrong. It's still not too late for him to walk away from this."

"I don't mind you talking, but if it's about us, then we deserve to know. Like we said…we don't want any heroes. We just want to collect our money and never see any of you again. You might think that we are wrong for doing this. God might condemn us for our actions here today. I don't care. I've tried to go about it with peace. We've finally had enough. We can't always be waiting for our turn to come around. We need to do something on our own." I could see that there was something underlying going on here and that it had to do with his *shtamm*.

We drove through this town like it was lost in time. Houses were literally destroyed with pieces of it still lying in debris all over the place. Kids were standing on the side of the road with their hands out and begging for food. It was not a sight to see with a full stomach. It affected myself, Jacob and all the others that had followed us into this bus.

"I can't believe I'm seeing this. It looks like this place was devastated and nobody did a damn thing to lift a finger to help." I didn't mean to say the exact same thing that was probably going through Mitchell's mind at this exact moment. He looked deep in thought and I could see his hardened expression on his face. "It doesn't look like anybody's been here in years."

"You're right, young lady and this place has all been but forgotten. It's not right and my friends and I are here to say that we're not going to take it anymore." The same pain that I had seen in Mitchell's eyes was now duplicated five times over through those that were following him. He was what I would consider a natural born leader, but he was using that unique ability in the wrong way. He should've been putting his effort into rebuilding. I did see that they had tried, but it appeared to me like nobody had the expertise to follow through.

"My wife and I can help rebuild. If you were to allow the others to go, we would stay and *schaffe* on your behalf." Jacob was trying to find a solution that would work for everybody. It appeared to me like it wasn't getting much traction. Mitchell was looking at him, but at the same time looking straight through him. "I'm a certified carpenter and Bethany is just about as good with a hammer, as I am, maybe more so. We would gladly stay behind and do this, because it's the right thing to do."

"My husband is only trying to give you another option. You could just stop all of this, ask for our help and we would gladly supply it. If you'd only come to us in the first place, we would've been able to save you all of this hardship. I still say that you have to look toward your Bible and find comfort in his words. It's the only way that you can truly get past all of this. He doesn't give you anything that you can't handle.

"You would do that for us? With nothing in return, you would bend over backwards to help us in our hour of need? I find that hard to believe. If you don't mind, I will stay the same course that I've been on from the very beginning." As we rolled down the track, we came to this barn that was barely standing. The roof had almost collapsed and the door was hanging off its hinges. They put the bus inside then they made us all get out and lie down with our faces planted in the hay.

They searched us, hoping that they would find something of use, like jewelry or some kind of momento that we held dear and cost a fortune. Unfortunately, they could only find trinkets that weren't worth very much, except that they were priceless to us.

He was getting frustrated and I could see it in his eyes. "All of these people and there are no damn rings or anything."

"I hate to be the bearer of bad news, but Amish Communities don't have any of those trappings. There are no such things as wedding rings or engagement rings for that matter. We go by the rule of the *zeugnis*. It's a bond that is made by a *mann* to the woman that he intends to be betrothed to. We abide by that with a ceremony that is meant to make us as one." I didn't want to throw water on his parade, but he had seriously taken things a little too far.

Chapter 6

He took one last ditch attempt and grabbed both me and Jacob and brought us outside to have a private conversation. "In all of these people, you can't tell me that there isn't something that we can use to help my people. I've given you access to a phone and it's time that you reach out to your family's.

"I don't think that we can do that. If we were to do that, we would make them into basket cases. We don't want them to worry, especially when they can't even do anything to help us in the first place. They have no money, no earthly possessions other than their land. You really didn't think this through, Mitchell." He was waving the gun in the air again and slapping his forehead with the palm of his hand. In his frustration, he inadvertently lowered his mask and now we were able to see his face.

"I can't let my people down. I can't let them see that this was for nothing. They would never look at me the same way again and I would probably lose all of their respect."

"I think that they would respect you more for cutting your losses. That way you can live to fight another day. Maybe find some other unwitting victims or possibly even take a different course altogether. My wife and I have given you what you really want. You need expertise and some way to show your people how to hold a hammer. We're willing to stay here, but you are just too damn stubborn to realize a good thing when it's staring you in the face." I didn't figure it was a good idea to antagonize him, but Jacob was losing his patience and that wasn't an easy thing for him to do.

"I don't like your attitude, Jacob. You think that you are better than me and I'm getting a little sick and tired of you sticking your nose where it doesn't belong. Maybe it's time that I take things to the next level. I didn't want to do this, but I had a feeling like it might come to this eventually. One of you is going to have to be sacrificed, so that the rest of them will understand just how serious this is. They will then be able to plead their case with

38

their family's with the anguish and tears still very fresh in their heart. That desperation will feed into the anxiety of their families. They will bend over backwards to get me that $10,000 from each household." He was quite brilliant, but his way of violence was only going to end in disaster.

"I still don't understand why your town was left out of the humanitarian aid workers program. The Red Cross or any of those other organizations are all over the place, so why wouldn't you just reach out to one of them."

"Bethany, don't you think we've tried that? Every time we try to get help, our advances are rebuffed. We don't even get an audience with any of those organizations. Somebody is trying to keep us down and we think it has something to do with those men that come by once a month to collect their fee for protection. It all started after the quake. These men would come by telling us anything we wanted to hear in exchange for our fealty. We give them practically everything we have, including food and provisions. In exchange, they keep the bandits and marauders from coming here. They have even promised to help rebuild…starting with the church.

I'm just not sure anymore that they're doing what's best for our people. I think they've played us for fools"

"I know that this might be hard to hear, but I don't think that this *mann* or his people are doing what's best for your people. I think you are starting to realize that now, because you've already started taking hostages. My husband Jacob is not wrong and what you need most is somebody to come here and teach you how to do these things on your own. You don't need to constantly bend over backwards for someone that doesn't do a damn thing in return."

"I'm beginning to think that you might be right. In order for us to truly find freedom, we have to do this ourselves. I'm going to need to make an example and it pains me to do so. I think that your people will show me the kind of fear that I need with your death, Bethany. I know that this doesn't seem fair, but what is fair nowadays? I need to think what's best for the many instead of the few. Your sacrifice will not be in vain and you will give a new life to this community.

"I don't think that you're going to lay a hand on her. You don't want to hurt anybody and I can see the pain in your eyes from even thinking about it. There is another way. You're smart enough to see it for yourself. We've already given you the tools and now you have to learn to pick it up and use them. You can look at it in two ways. One is that you will finally be able to give your people what they deserve and two, you'll finally able to roll up your sleeves and get a handle on your life." He didn't want to hear this. He didn't want to be seen as somebody that had to be told what to do. He wanted to be the hero and the only way that was going to happen was if he was to show them that he was not going to back down.

Whoever this new player in town that was making their life miserable was certainly putting this kid on a track that was only going to end with his own death. I don't think that either Jacob or I could live with ourselves if that were to happen. We had to make him see that he could make a difference without violence and death at every turn. It was time for him to stand up and be a *mann* and stop acting like a little boy. He didn't have to wait for this *mann* and his people to deliver. They could do it themselves and tell this *mann* to shove it.

In all time that we had been here, we did hear rumors that there were people that were trying to profit from this disaster. We really couldn't believe it, but now that we were seeing it with our own eyes, there was nothing like real proof to show you that humanity could be its own worst enemy.

Chapter 7

"Mitchell, you are obviously religious. We can see how dedicated to your people you are. That is admirable, but what you're doing is not. What would God want for your people? Would he want you to hold a gun in his name? Would he want you to kill in his name? Of course not, he would want you to do what was right and not what's easy. The easy thing to do is to extort money through violence. You can't think that fighting fire with fire is a good idea. My husband and I have always turned the other cheek. We look for the good in people and we know that we can see that in you. God can see that in you. He watches you all the time and he knows that deep down you are a good person."

I was trying to make him realize that God did not walk away from them. He was the one that walked away from his faith and it was time that he finally found it again. I could see in his eyes that he wasn't happy with any of this. He saw no choice and it was like the answer that he was seeking came to him in a blinding moment of clarity. He had lost his way and it was up to me and my husband to show him the way back onto the path that was supposed to be his.

"I've tried and I've tried and every time I get slapped down by the man. I always thought the same way that you did and that God would always have my back. After this disaster, I felt like he didn't think that we were worthy of his love and guidance. I gave it every effort to find that spark of goodness, but it was marred by this man and his people that came looking for a handout. We knew that they were serious and that we couldn't just send them on their way. They wouldn't take no for an answer. I don't even think there are marauders or bandits out there. I think they just made that up, but we saw that they meant what they said and they were willing to back it up with guns. It was just a good thing that I followed them one day. I got my hands on some of their weapons."

He was holding it in his hand, looking at it from all angles and it was like he was seeing power for the first time in his life.

"Mitchell, I want you to know that holding that thing doesn't give you the right kind of strength. It does give you a strength, but it's not the right kind. You need to lay down your weapons. You need to walk away from this before this gets out of hand. We can convince our people that you were out of your mind. We can even convince them not to mention a word of this to anybody. We just don't know how much longer it will be before they try to take matters into their own hands. Nerves are frayed and people are on edge. You need to do the right thing and we both know what that is. If you don't know, then I suggest that you look at these verses. They might make you see for the first time." I opened my Bible to those verses that were underlined in yellow.

I placed it in his hands and he looked at it like it was a foreign thing that was going to burst him into flames. He probably thought that he was evil and that he didn't deserve to even look upon the pages. "I've been down this road before, Bethany and it never leads to anything that's good and honest. All these words do is raise more questions than answers. We know that we're not the only ones that this group has decided to target. They pick on those communities that are out of reach and barely standing on their own. We don't have much and they take whatever we have and it has to stop. I plan to confront them the next time they come around and believe me they better listen to reason or else."

"Are you listening to yourself, Mitchell. Of course, those men don't deserve your respect, but they don't deserve to die by your hand either. You must know that deep down. There has to be a semblance of something that was lost to you from the moment of this devastation. We see it for ourselves and there is goodness and all you have to do is look for it."

"I don't think you understand and my people have gone through enough and we just can't take it anymore. They need me to show them that there is something that we can do about it. We don't have to just stand there and take that kind of abuse willingly and readily." He was getting fired up and that was the one thing that I was hoping would happen. It might open his eyes to the reality of the situation and not to the fantasy that he had been conjuring up in his head.

"I know that you don't see any way out of this, but trust me, Bethany and I can help you. We are literally sacrificing our time with our *shtamm* to help you. It would be better that it came from you. I don't really think that you need anybody. Each and every one of you that make this place a home has the ability to work with their hands. Hard *schaffe* is not something and you should walk away from. It gives character, a sense of purpose and makes you think that you are overcoming the odds."

"Jacob, you make a valid argument. I'm sure that there are some of my people that can do that. Money isn't really for rebuilding and it's for more weapons. We need to fight back against this man that thinks that he can take what we have with nothing in return. I'm through talking about this and it's time for me to do something that will make people stand up and take notice. Your friends will finally know what it means to feel desperation and loss." He went to grab me and his hand was now clasped on to my wrist. I got this instant feeling of dread. It was as if my life was passing before my eyes.

Chapter 8

"Carl, bring the hostages out here. I have something for them to see. This should finally make them realize that I'm not just talking to hear myself think." His hand was still holding on to my wrist and I tried to wrestle free, but it was like trying to get away from a ravaging grizzly bear.

The door to the barn opened and I heard the scuffling of feet and murmurs of those that I called friend. "I said everybody get out here. Our leader would like to have a few words." I could hear something that wasn't there before. This was determination and apparently Carl was now seeing his leader, as somebody that wasn't weak and in over his head.

"This woman means a lot to all of you. I'm going to put a bullet into the back of her head." Mitchell said it with such ice in his tone that I believed him right down to my very bones. "I don't take any joy in this. Unfortunately, you don't see me as somebody to take seriously. I'm not opposed to violence and you're about to find out that I can be ruthless and without mercy." He was dragging me in the dirt, my dress getting dirty and my knees getting scraped up along the way.

"You don't have to do this and Bethany and I have given you another way. All you have to do is take it, grab our hand and we will gladly show you what needs to be done. It's the best that we can do and I would think that you would grab onto the lifeline that we are throwing you." I could see that Jacob was worried and he was trying to fix things. It's just that Mitchell wasn't really in the frame of mind to listen. He had everybody's undivided attention and he didn't want anything to happen to lose it. "I really don't think that you've given what we had to talk about any thought. You should really talk to your people and find out if there are others that are thinking along the same way as we are."

"I'm the one that tells them what to think. You are a hostage and it's time that you start acting like it. Maybe when I put your wife in the ground that you're finally realize that this isn't just smoke and mirrors. I mean what I say and I say what I mean. I would gladly allow you to take her place, but I don't think that you're going to be man enough to stand up and do something like that." He obviously did not know my husband well enough to say something like that, because he was about to find out that Jacob had a lot more conviction than anybody that I had ever known in my life.

"I will gladly take her place. You can put me on my knees and you can blow the back of my head off. Just leave her alone. She is more important to me than my own life. Maybe if somebody was that important to you that you would understand that. My life is nothing without her." His hand was on the gun and he had me kneeling with my head bowed forward. I closed my eyes hoping to God that I would not hear the trigger being pulled. "I mean it; I will gladly take her place if that's what it takes to get my wife out of this in one piece.'

"I can't believe that you would even consider something like that. She honestly means the world to you. I guess I don't know what that kind of love is like. I used to, but he walked away when things got tough. He disappeared when we needed him the most. Instead, we had to deal with the devil." I could see out of my peripheral vision that each and every one of his people were now nodding in compliance.

"I don't want my husband to take my place and I hope to God that you don't take him at his word. He means the world to me and I don't think that I could live without him." I'd now put him into a corner; and what do animals usually do when they are cornered?

"I don't care who I put the bullet into, but somebody is going to show these others that we are not just here for show. This is not some kind of bluff." He pushed me away from him with the boot of his right front. He grabbed Jacob, kicked him in the back of the leg and made him kneel at his feet.

I scrambled on my hands and knees backwards, looking at him holding the gun. There was hardness in his features, something that made me believe that he would follow through on his promise. I wanted to do something. It was in the hands of God himself.

Chapter 9

I was terrified beyond words. Mitchell had his gun pressed up against my husband's head. His finger leveled on the trigger. If I didn't do something, he would surely go through with this. I had to do something. It was time to take the fight to his people. It was obvious that Mitchell wasn't listening, so maybe they would. If I could change their minds, then it might mean that he would finally see that all life was precious.

I stood up, not even bothering to dust myself off. I implored my case to the rest of them. "You can't possibly think that this is the right thing to do. It's wrong and I think that deep down you know that. He's only doing this to show you that he is a leader. I don't think he needs to do that to make you see him as a leader. What he needs to do is to make a good example. He can't do that with you all looking for him for guidance. He thinks that he needs to do this in order to give you a sense of hope for the future. You don't want this and I can see it written all over your faces. Tell him for

God's sake; before he does something that he can never walk away from. It's not too late and somebody is going to have to stand up and be noticed."

"I'm sorry; Bethany, but my people don't see it the same way. They need me to stand up for them. If I don't, then those men and the man that they report to are going to walk all over them. We can't have that. We are barely able to survive without giving to them every time that they roll into town once a month. I'm tired of it, my people are tired of it and we are the only few that have been willing to do anything about it" The only thing I could find solace in any of this was that he didn't pull the trigger yet.

"My wife is right and there is a better way. You can still fight back, but do it in peace. You can't possibly believe that this is the right way. You all can think for yourselves. You don't need him to lead you by the hand. Stand up and do something that gives your life meaning. Let us show you how to do that." His gun was shaking in his hand. He really didn't want to go through with this.

"Mitchell, you don't have to do this for me." Carl was the first one to show any kind of resolve. "I've been listening to all of this and they make sense. They don't have to help us, but they are doing it out of the goodness of their hearts. They've even given us a way to learn to do these things on our own. They're willing to stay around. How many people have even given us the time of day? They might be trying to trick us, but I don't see any kind of dishonesty coming from either one of them." They were all dressed the same in that they were wearing black, but Carl was brave enough to take off his mask.

Once he did that, the others followed suit me and before long they were all standing and looking at Mitchell. They had pleaded our case for us, but not until we had shown them that they could have something different.

Chapter 10

"Fine, if all of you agree, then I will put down the gun." He lowered his weapon to the ground. The others did the exact same thing. I went over to have a counsel with my friends. I told them that he was lost and that we had been able to help him find his way. He needed our understanding. We didn't have to get the law involved, but they had to make that decision for themselves. This is something that was going to have to come from their own good graces. This was something that was going to be decided among to them and not just as a group, but as individuals.

Jacob stood on shaky legs and you could see that he was very affected by what had happened. "You made the right decision, Mitchell...let's get started on that future we promised you."

In the next few hours, we found out that there were at least three of them that had a pretty good knowledge of what it was like to build things with their own hands. They usually made wood carvings. They were able to translate that into hammering in a nail and erecting a building. We drove back into town and before we knew it, we had several of the locals lending a hand. It was an amazing sight to see. It did my heart proud to know that we had shown them that there was hope. All they had to do was look in the right place to find it.

It was unanimous and those on the bus had decided that they would keep their mouths shut. The story was concocted that the bus had broken down and even the bus driver had decide to go along with it.

"I really think that your people are getting the hang of this." It was something to see them working hand in hand for a common goal. "Instead of using violence, you are using what God gave you in abundance. You have skills and all you have to do is learn to trust one another. It's not just a matter of having expertise, but it's also knowing where your strengths and weaknesses are. You can build on that. I've seen that with my own eyes. You really have shown me that we were right to know that there was a spark there. We just had to fan it into a flame. Now you have that desire burning through your veins. You don't want to just contain yourself with your own community. You want to branch out and make life better for others."

"Bethany, you are exactly right and I now know that what I have been doing was wrong. I should've seen the goodness. It's just that these men and the one that they follow are making everybody doubt themselves. We feel like we are downtrodden. We'll never feel like that again. As God is my witness, I will make this community live again. I even looked into bringing back the word of God. Our minister was very glad to see us back within the flock. He has been busily telling us what you have recently made us see. He just didn't have the conviction that the both of you have."

"Bethany might forgive your trespasses, Mitchell, but I will never forget the way that gun felt against the back of my head. I hope that you never have to do anything like that again. No *mann* should feel like their life is over before it begins. You're just starting and you have a long road to go before this country of yours is back on its feet. With people like you leading the charge, I have no doubt that things are in good hand. We will come back soon to find that you have made a real difference. Trust in yourself and the rest will follow in the goodness of humanity. Maybe that will help you reach out to others."

"I'm going to escort you back to the airport. I can only go about a mile, before we'll have to turn back before being discovered. My friends and those of my family and the people in this community thank you. If it wasn't for you, I might have turned to my darker side. I'm glad that you were able to make my people see it from your point of view. We will continue your good work that you started. We will go to other communities in peace and try to get them out from underneath the tyranny of this man. They call him El Diablo. It means the devil, but we now know that there is no such thing. There is evil, but we will fight it every step of the way."

He was a *mann* of his word and he did take us to the airport. He left us to tell the authorities what happened and everybody had the exact same tale from beginning to end.

They couldn't find any holes in our story and there was another aircraft inbound to take us back home. Mitchell and his band of merry men will keep on fighting the good fight. We would come back and look in on them. It is the least that we can do. If anything, we could stop in and see how his community is faring. He had left behind two of his people, just in case those marauders or El Diablo as he put it came calling again. This time, they would come up against resistance. Maybe that was all that it would take to make them walk away or run away in the opposite direction.

We were in the plane and looking out and before long we were Airborne. I grabbed my husband's hand and I made a sigh of relief, until suddenly there was this whoosh. Flames began to spread quickly all over the outside of the aircraft. We were literally on fire, a fireball going down the runway and we had just lifted. We were now coming back down the hard way.

BOOK 6

Chapter 1

I thought that I was imagining things, but that fire was very real. In fact, Jacob was now standing and those that had come onto the plane with us were now panicking. There had to be a reason for this, but what that was, was anybody's guess. For now, I couldn't satisfy myself with knowing who had done this and my main concern was getting everybody off the plane safely.

The plane crashed landing back onto the tarmac and the sickening crunch of metal hitting pavement was almost too much to bear. We were jolted out of our seats and those flames were still licking at the windows. I peered out to see only a ball of orange and then I noticed that the airplane wasn't the only thing on fire.

"Jacob, I think you've got to see this." He followed my gaze and he looked at me with great concern and we both saw that the airport was also on fire. "Somebody really doesn't want us to leave and is trying to make it impossible for us to make our way back to our *shtamm*."

"Bethany, as God is my witness I will get you back to your *dochtah*." We could hear people yelling and the stewardess was trying to calm people down, but was having less than any good luck. "For now, we have to remain calm. Let's try to get these people to realize that not everything is lost." I thought that that was a good idea, considering that you could see that most people were not thinking clearly. If given a choice, they would trample over their young to get out of the plane. It was too bad that they didn't have a level head like myself and Jacob or the several other Amish people from other communities that had taken flight with us.

"Please, everybody calm down and follow me to the exits. The one that we're using is at the back of the plane where there are no flames. Just line up. I said line up and don't push or shove; everybody will have a chance to get out." This stewardess was having a hard time dealing with all of these people. I gave her credit for trying, but the plane was small by conventional standards.

I got up and Jacob followed suit and we stood with her in a sign of solidarity. "I want you to listen to the stewardess, because she is only trying to help. You can't run around with your head cut off. We have to follow the one leading and right now that's the stewardess." Jacob had his hand raised and immediately everybody shut up like he was giving them reason to hope. The smoke in the cabin was getting pretty thick. The flames had not reached the inside, but it was just a matter of time. You could smell the acrid odor of burnt rubber and metal melting outside.

"If you listen to my husband, then you'll get out of here and back to your loved ones. If you listen in the distance, you can hear the sirens coming. They are coming to help us." I didn't hear any sirens, but that false hope gave them relief from the constant worry of being burned alive. "I need the women and children to come to the front and the men to follow from behind." They were actually taking direction, because in their minds they really did believe that they could hear the sirens. It was because they wanted to believe that there were sirens and that there were people coming to help.

The stewardess, a Haitian local named Leanne whispered into my ear "I'm so thankful for your help and I don't know if I could've kept them calm long enough to find a way out. Only problem is, I don't know if there is a way out. I'm trying to keep myself from panicking, but the only exit that is viable is in the back and I think that is wishful thinking."

"I'm glad that you said something, but we have to check it out regardless." I followed her and Jacob followed me and we went to that exit, only to touch the surface of the door and feel the heat burning my fingertips. I took it back and looked at her and told her without saying anything that we couldn't open this door without risk of being flash fried.

"This isn't good and we have to tell them something. They're looking for us for guidance. They want us to have the answers. I'm just not sure they're going to like what we have to say. If either one of you have any ideas, I would love to hear them right about now. I can't get in touch with the cabin or the crew. The captain has remained silent and I think that he's either injured or dead."

Whoever had trained her in managing stress had done a wonderful job.

"I want everybody to look out a window that you see and tell me what you are looking at. If it's just fire, then don't bother to report back, but if there's something else, then I want to hear about it." Jacob was the voice of reason and even though they were mumbling with dissension, they followed without question or hesitation. Each and every one of them began to look out the windows, turning with disgust and fear on their faces.

I looked out of one side of the plane and I noticed something. This part of the plane had no flames and then I saw a miraculous sight that made me smile. Outside away from the plane were Mitchell and his people doing what they could to put out the flames with buckets of water.

"I think we have a reason to hope."

Chapter 2

"Is that who I think it is, Bethany?" All I could do was nod my head to Jacob and hug him, not fully realizing that we were not completely out of danger yet. "I can't believe that he stayed behind. I thought for sure that he was going to leave. He was supposed to find out who this El Diablo character is and put a stop to him once and for all. I'm not saying that I'm not glad to see him. Without him, I don't think that we would have had a chance to survive."

I turned and put my hands up for everybody to listen. Nearly everybody looked towards me. "I think we have saviors that are risking their own lives to come to our rescue. It's not the police or the fire department. These men are doing this because it's the right thing to do. We need to follow their example. The exit on this side of the plane is the only way. The stewardess will wait for my signal and then I will tell her when to open those doors."

"What makes you think that you are the leader of all of us?" There would always be one in every crowd. This guy stepped forward and look like the big shot. "I'm an ex navy cadet. I should be the one that's taking control the situation." He could say that now, but he was just as much in a panic as everybody else was a few minutes ago. "I don't think that we should use that exit. You just touched it and it was hot." That was before Mitchell started to rain down water from not only buckets, but now a hose had come into play.

"My wife and I really do appreciate your concern, but I think we have everything well in hand. This exit is the only one that we can use. If we try any other ones, we're going to get burned alive." Nobody had mentioned those few that had died on impact. They were lying there in their own blood. There were even a couple of injured that were moaning for some kind of assistance. "What you can do is take a couple people and help those that are too hurt to get up on their own 2 feet." I thought for sure that he was going to argue with my husband, but he decided against it. I think it was because he noticed that everybody was following

Jacob. To take that attention away from us was only going to make things more difficult.

I will say that he did have a leadership kind of quality. He grabbed two young men and they looked like they could handle themselves. They could help those that had broken bones or lacerations. A first aid kit was passed around and those wounds that could be cared for were seen to.

"I don't think that this one is in any shape to do anything. He's unconscious, bleeding from the nose and mouth, but he does have a pulse." Now that everybody had duties to perform, it made it easier to keep them from realizing that the fire was still out there. It was ready at any moment to come in here and do what nature intended it to do. "I've applied pressure to the wounds on his face, but I really think that he's going to need a Dr. He was pretty good with a first aid kit and I could see that his training in the navy was coming into play.

There were at least five that were dead and it wasn't hard to see that their necks were broken. Their vacant eyes were looking back at us. The most likely broke their necks trying to stand up when the plane was going down. They would be the last ones to leave the plane, but nobody was going to be left behind.

I saw that the flames had diminished where the exit was. I gave a perceptible nod towards Leanne. She gave one back and then turned the latch on the door and kicked it open. The slide came out of nowhere. It inflated and I could see one of Mitchell's men down below ready to catch any one that was coming down. The women, children and injured went first and then everybody else followed suit. Finally Jacob and myself helped the dead, before leaving ourselves.

"What the damn happened?"

I wasn't exactly comfortable with the way that he was swearing, but I suppose I could understand under the circumstance.

"We really don't know, but we're very grateful to see you, Mitchell. I guess God was working through you. Had he not been, then you would not be here and I don't think any of us would be either." This time, I did hear sirens in the distance.

It appeared that help and medical personnel were on the way.

"Bethany, I don't know anything about that, but I do know that this was no accident. I could smell the gasoline when I got here and I was just lucky that it hadn't spread too far around the plane. I was able to hold it back with water. I don't like this and it's an awfully big coincidence to have this happen. We were about to embark on a peace delegation." As if answer to his query, a red dot appeared on his chest and then I heard somebody screaming and then Carl jumped in front of Mitchell. A crack of thunder and this red pool appeared on his chest. He fell backwards into Mitchell's arms.

He began dragging him away, as the pavement began to take on pock marks from some kind of sniper that couldn't be seen. We followed him with his men. I looked back to see that others were walking around quite confused. It appeared that Mitchell was the target and then he was helping his dead friend into the back of a truck with a canvas cover over the back. We joined them and then the truck began to peel rubber. We were anything but safe. I heard a motor thinking it was a vehicule of the fire department. They had arrived on the scene. But it turned out that that was not what I heard. I saw the jeep with men with guns chasing us.

Chapter 3

"I hate to be the bearer of bad news, Mitchell, but we have company. Whoever these guys are I can only assume that it has something to do with El Diablo. He's not letting us get away easily. They probably thought that they had us dead to rights on the plane. I would say that you're not their only target. If I were to hazard a guess, I would say that Jacob and I are on their hit parade as well. It would make sense, considering that we did help you decide to fight for yourselves. To build with your own bare hands and not take charity from others."

"Bethany, I'm very grateful for everything that you and Jacob have done, but I was hoping to get you out of the line of fire. That's not going to be an easy thing to do. I want you to know that I will protect you with my life, like Carl has done for me. He shouldn't have done that. I never told him that I wanted his undying loyalty."

"I think that I can speak for Bethany and myself, Mitchell. These men feel a kinship towards you and they know that you have been the one to show them the way. You might have been ill advised to take hostages but your intentions were good. They were just marred by desperation. I think that your driver should try and lose this jeep, as soon as possible." I heard bullets being fired and the canvas tarp over the truck took the brunt of the attack. We dove for cover and lay flat on the metal floor, listening to the angry voices from outside getting closer.

"My best man Rafael is driving and he knows this area like the back of his hand. We grew up around here together and we got into a lot of trouble and were able to outwit the authorities by knowing all the little paths that they didn't know about. He's going to have to find one of them. We won't be able to outrun them in this lumbering vehicle." This was not the same bus that we had come in. They had absconded with a truck that was found nearby. It might've been illegal, but it was a necessary evil.

"I hope you're right, Mitchell. That jeep it is not going to go away willingly."

"I think I know how they set your plane on fire. I think that I can fight fire with fire." There were two Gas Containers by the back door attached to the wall and he began to unscrew them and check the contents. One was half full and the other one was empty. He took the one that was half full, unscrewed the cap and ripped off a piece of his shirt. He stuffed it into the hole. He took out a lighter, lit the makeshift fuse and then walked to the back. He motioned for one of his men to open the flap. When he did, he tossed the contents towards the jeep that was in hot pursuit.

I didn't hear anything for a moment, but then the explosion was enough to make all of us cringe. I heard the sound of brakes, squealing on rubber and then what sounded like a vehicle crash into a tree.

"That was pretty quick thinking, Mitchell. You really do know how to think on your feet. They are definitely not going to be able to follow us in that heap. It doesn't mean that they won't call for reinforcements. We should get off the road when your guy decides to do that." Jacob was just finishing her speech, when Mitchell started to climb outside of that truck and disappeared from view. I saw a silhouette of his frame moving across the canvas and then he disappeared. I thought for a moment that he had fallen, but then that truck began to take a different route.

I could hear the smacking of the tree branches hitting that truck. We came to a complete stop about 20 minutes later.

When we get out, there was this old abandoned building that looked like an orphanage sitting in disrepair. "This is where we're going to stay for the night. We'll get a fresh start in the morning. We don't want to be on the roads, until this heat dies down." It was an apt metaphor, considering the frying pan and the fire that we had just gotten out of.

We helped those that came with us. We had a motley crew of survivors that decided against their better judgment to follow us. The *mann* with the navy training went along for the ride, along with two women and another *mann* that looked like he was in a state of shock. We gathered them inside, finding that there was no hot water, no water to speak of whatsoever and it appeared that the place was abandoned.

We settled down for the night with candles that were found in a nearby kitchen. We were settling in, when we heard voices. I looked at Mitchell and he grabbed his gun and myself and Jacob followed him. We came across five children huddled in a corner by an older man. Mitchell put his hand on the man's wrist and looked at me and shook his head to indicate that there was no way that he would see another day.

It appeared that we not only had a motley crew to take care of, but now we had five children. All of this was getting a little out of hand.

I'd learned some of the French dialect, while I was here these couple of months. I found the language to be very easy to understand and I talked to the children and found out that the man was Jerome and he was their guardian. They were now without an adult to take care of them. One young man named Francois or more commonly known as Frankie was very quiet and was glaring at us with daggers. None of these kids look like they were willing to listen to us. It reminded me of my own *dochtah*, she was always a little precocious and curious for her own good.

Chapter 4

"I don't like this and it's bad enough that I have to look after the both of you, plus those others that followed. Now you expect me to take care of children. I don't think you know this about me, but children and I don't mix well. It's better that we leave them here. They're safer on their own. Did you forget that El Diablo is looking for us at this very moment? His men are going to comb this area and it's not going to be long before they find this place."

"I can't believe that I'm hearing this from you, Mitchell. You can't possibly believe that they're better off alone. They are children for God's sake and they deserve more respect than that. We have no choice. You can leave if you want to, but Jacob and I are staying to look after these children." I was standing my ground, my hands on my hips and he was about to say something in rebuttal, but then he thought better of it.

Instead of saying anything at all, he threw up his hands in disbelief that we would even consider something like this. He had resigned himself to staying with us. He told his men, only to get them to go along with this insanity. When he became adamant, there were raised voices, but then they fell into line.

"Bethany, are you sure that we can handle this? They're not exactly easy to get along with. Frankie seems to be the ringleader. The rest of them are following his lead and he's telling them not to trust us. I guess I can understand where he's coming from. We're essentially strangers and the only people that they really saw as their savior was Jerome. I noticed that he's not a local and I would say that he came here to open up this place. He died before he was able to do any renovations with the little budget that he probably had."

"I don't know about anything, Jacob. I just don't think it's right that we leave these kids. I've seen how kids live without parental guidance and it's like Lord of the flies." I'd come across that book and I found the story to be intense. I was interesting enough to keep me on the edge of my seat. You probably don't know what I'm talking about. I told you that you should read the book, but you were dead set against it. Anyway, they acted like wild animals. I can't in good conscience just walk away."

"Bethany, you are very strong and stubborn and I think that is the reason why I married you. Just be careful, because Frankie cannot be trusted. He's bitter and angry and is ready to lash out at anybody that comes into his personal space." I already saw that for myself. I tried to give him some of my bottled water, but he looked at me like I was trying to poison them. He had long hair that hadn't been washed in days and his face was covered in mud. He had the kids huddled in a corner. They were talking in hushed tones and were making sure that we couldn't hear a word that was being said.

"I think I convinced Mitchell that we can't leave without them. I know that he won't leave without us. It's a vicious cycle, but that serves the purpose." I managed to find some blankets and I handed them out to the kids. There were a little hesitant, but then Frankie gave his nod of approval and then they were eager to comply. The one thing that they wouldn't do was drink anything that we offered them or eat any of the food that we had in our possession. I'd actually managed to convince customs that I could bring these vegetables on board.

To show them that it wasn't poisoned, I took a bite out of each thing. They then had the fortitude to take it from my hands. Their wild eyes were looking at me the entire time and it was making me feel like I was on display.

I left them and found Jacob talking to Mitchell "I'm sorry for your *mann*. Carl was a good *mann* and he was the one that made everybody realized that you didn't have to kill me to make your point. Just know that his loss is felt right here in my heart and I know that Bethany feels the same way."

"I appreciate all that, but I really don't have time to grieve. There is no water and our supplies are limited. At the crack of dawn, I am going to make a run to a stream that I can hear nearby. Two of my men are doing some reconnaissance. We don't want to be surprised by unwelcome visitors." I nodded my head and I could see that he was really growing into his role as a leader.

"I hate to interrupt, but I want to introduce myself." We all turned and saw this man with a shaved head. He was the cadet from the plane, who had helped treat the injured. "I'm Sean. I just want you to know that I wasn't trying to usurp your authority back there in the plane. I just thought we needed somebody with leadership. Apparently you do that by a natural ability. I'm going to go out and meet up with a couple of your men, Mitchell." He nodded and then he disappeared through the door, leaving us to wonder what our next move was.

"You two have been nothing but a headache, since the moment that I met you on that bus. If you insist on bringing the children, then we are going to have to lay a low here for a couple of days. If we're seen on the road with children, it will be like putting a neon sign on our backs."

Chapter 5

"I don't know what to do, Jacob. These kids don't trust anybody but their dead guardian and Frankie. They don't do anything without his approval. I've become a taste tester, just so that they know that I am not trying to kill them."

"Bethany, you just answered your own question. If you want them to trust you, then you have to get the trust of Frankie before anybody else. You need to reach out to him and I'll help you, but for most part this is going to have to be a *maemm's* intuition. You've dealt with your own *dochtah*. I'm sure that she has not been all sunshine and lollipops all the time. There had to be a moment that you felt like you had to lay down the law. Instead of chastising her, you convinced her that you were only looking out for her best interest." I should've realized the answer myself, but I needed Jacob to smack me across the face with it.

"You're right and my *dochtah* has been a handful at times. Even my *maemm* in law has had her problems dealing with her. I talked to them the other day and for the most part they have been living in harmony together. I told her in no uncertain terms that she was not to lay a hand on my *dochtah*. She can give her timeouts, or take away from her privileges, but in no way is she to touch her with any kind of corporal punishment. I think that I can use what I've learned with my *dochtah* on Frankie and the rest of the kids." I was considering bribery with candy, but that was a last resort.

"I don't want you to say anything. I just want you to listen to what I have to tell you." They looked terrified out of their minds. They gathered around Frankie, as their one and only protector. "I understand that all of you are scared and that we are strangers and shouldn't be trusted. I don't know what to tell you. I'm sorry for the loss of your guardian, Jerome. He must've been very important to you. I'm sure that Frankie has been quite instrumental in keeping you all together. If you're afraid that we're going to break you apart, then you have nothing to worry about."

"Lady, you have no idea what we've been through. I don't think that you're here out of the goodness of your hearts. We overheard some of your men talking about El Diablo." That kind of information couldn't be kept under wraps for long. I sat down in the Lotus position with my long dress fanned out around me. The *kinner* looked at me with mistrust.

"You shouldn't have heard that and it's not right to eavesdrop. However, since you did, I think that I owe you the truth. El Diablo and his men have decided to target Mitchell, my husband and myself. We believe that he wants to kill us and we took refuge in here. It was never our intention to put any of you in danger. We can't leave you here. There's no telling what they would do if they found you. To that end, we are taking you with us." There were murmurs of disapproval and Frankie was now holding them back with his hands.

"I don't think that your fight is ours. If you were to leave here right now and not look back, then you wouldn't have the worry about us getting hurt. You may not think that we can take care of ourselves, but we can. Each and every day, I go down to the stream and retrieve water for all of us. I hunt during

86

the day. I've even learned to fish and cook on the stove, courtesy of Jerome. He was the only one that cared for us after all of this began." He was like a wall and I was chipping away at the surface with nothing, but my fingernails.

"OK, I was trying to be nice, but I don't think you understand. You are in danger and you're coming with us whether you want to or not. Just make sure that you're ready when the time comes. We won't be leaving for a couple of days and for the time being, you're just going to have to put up with us." I didn't mean to lay down the law, but they weren't responding to kid gloves. It was time to take them off.

"You're upsetting my friends. We need to talk this over in private. I think that you can at least give us that kind of respect." He was showing himself to be older than his age of 12 years. He had wisdom that came from surviving on the streets. I backed away and went out the door to give them time to take everything into consideration.

"I heard everything that you said to him. I imagine that it wasn't easy for you to lay down the law.

They are *kinner* and we have to protect them, even if it means making them feel a little bit uncomfortable in our presence. You're a good wife and *maemm*. You should trust your instincts more often. I saw the way that you were with the *kinner* back at the camp. I was quite impressed. I don't think we've talked about this, but I think that I would like a *bobli*. I know that the timing is wrong and talking about something like this right now seems like the future and so far away."

"I have been thinking about the same thing, Jacob, but I think that we should hold off for the time being. We still have a lot to do."

"I know that we do, Bethany, but it's just something that I wanted you to know that I was thinking about it." I'd given them enough time and I walked in there to see that the *kinner* were alone. Frankie was gone. We came to the conclusion together that he probably ran away. Why these kids trusted him was beyond me.

Chapter 6

"The kids have gotten even more difficult without Frankie as their buffer. They are shaking like leaves and they won't even let me get close enough to talk to them. They won't take water or food and it doesn't matter if I taste it or not. They want Frankie back, but I think we both know that he's not coming back. He ran off. He was thinking about himself and nobody else."

"I know that you're angry with him, Bethany, but you can't deny that these kids have been through hell and that they've come out on the other side. You should know that I talked to Mitchell. His men have looked around the area, but have come up with nothing to indicate where Frankie went. If he really does know his way around, then there are nooks and crannies of all over this land that he could hide in. We may never find him. That's something that we're going to have to live with."

"I'm going to try one more time to get through to them. They just don't understand how dangerous it is for them to stay here. This place needs a lot of work and I don't know if it's safe for them to stay here any longer."

"Bethany, I'll take a couple of guys with me, including Sean and we'll try to keep this place from falling down around our ears. We won't be here that long, so anything that I do will be temporary. Mitchell has already heard from one of his men and they told him that El Diablo is not giving up his search. He has actually expanded it with more men and there's no way that we're going to be able to hide from whatever net they have put around this place. They will have roadblocks, but Mitchell has assured me that he knows of several other ways to avoid the main road. He's not very happy that we are taking five *kinner* along with his men and those that survived the aircraft."

"I think I understand. It would be better for him if it was just himself and his men. They could move quickly and wouldn't have us weighing him down like an anchor around his neck. I guess I have to give him credit for sticking around. He really didn't have to. There would be nothing that we could do to stop him if he wanted to leave. I think that he feels like he owes us something. I guess after putting a gun to your head and almost killing you, he does."

"Bethany, I was thinking the same thing and his guilt over almost taking my life has made him feel responsible for keeping us alive."

I stepped back into the room and the kids were now still looking at me like I was the devil incarnate. I tried to reach out for them, but they pulled away from me. They began to cry and thrash like stubborn *kinner* did when they didn't get their way. I tried again, only to have them slap at my hands and make me back away before things escalated any further.

"I know that this doesn't make any sense. Frankie has run off and left you to fend for yourselves. You're going to have to trust us to get you out of this place. Bad men are coming."

"You are the bad man and we don't trust anybody that has a gun." This was a little girl. I didn't even know her name, but now she was stepping up to take the place of Frankie. "We won't go with you and if you try to make us, we will make your life a living hell. We'll scream and whoever you are running from will hear us and then you won't be able to get away. You're better off leaving us here." She was right and if they did put up a fuss, they were going to become a nuisance that we just couldn't afford.

"I really don't have time for this, so you are going to have to tell me what it's going to take for you to come with us and be quiet about it." They turned to each other and began to talk like they had a secret that they didn't want me to hear. Their clothes were tattered, their little bodies malnourished. We had to get them to eat something more than just vegetables after we got out of here.

"We talked about it and we will go with you, but only if you leave your guns behind." Out of the mouths of babes; I had to try to convince Mitchell that he couldn't bring his weapons along. That was not going to be easy. I wasn't even sure if I was going to be able to accomplish such a feat.

I told Jacob what they said and he smiled and shook his head in disbelief. "I can't believe that they would say something like that. It amazes me what strange concepts they come up with at such an early age. I understand that they are afraid of guns, but it's the only protection that we have against an enemy that is willing to shoot us between the eyes. I don't want to use them myself, but I don't think that we're going to be able to walk away from this without Mitchell and his men guarding and keeping us safe. There's no way Mitchell is going to allow his men to drop their weapons, but maybe there is another way." He told me his plan and it was interesting how his mind worked. I had to smile thinking that my husband really did know what was best.

I went back in and the kids were looking at me and hoping that I was going to tell them exactly what they wanted to hear. "I've talked to them about the guns. They promise to leave them behind. They'll even let you see the hiding place of the weapons, before we get back on the truck and drive away from here." I think they were shocked, but not as shocked as I was by the words that were coming out of my mouth. I think they believed, but only because I had lied through my teeth. I didn't feel very good about it.

"We'll only believe what you say, after we've talked to the leader of those that have the guns." I should've realized that it wasn't going to be that easy.

Chapter 7

"Bethany, I admire the way that you convinced them to come with us. I have no problem getting my men to leave behind some of their weapons, but what you're asking me to do is impossible. I can't talk to them and I've never been able to connect with children. I think I already told you this, but I don't think I have made myself abundantly clear. I don't want anything to do with them and this is all on you. I'm not going to be responsible for their safety. My responsibility is to you and my men. That is as far as my good graces are going to extend." I didn't know why he was getting so angry, but something was obviously upsetting him.

"I don't see where all this is coming from. I'm only asking you to talk to them and convince them that its time for them to leave. All you really have to do is tell them that you're going to put down your guns. They just want to hear it from the leader. I don't think that's too much to ask for." He was rubbing his scalp, holding his hand over his head and pacing back and forth in frustration.

"I don't want to and I don't think I have to. They are freaking children and they should be paying attention and not acting like brats. Just tell them anything to get them to fall in line. I know it's not easy; believe me I've had my fair share dealing with kids that didn't want to do what they were told." Now I was getting to the meat of the matter. Something had obviously happened when he was younger to make him this nervous around kids. "I can't even look at them." I could see that. He hadn't spent any time with them from the moment that we had arrived a day ago.

"I think that you would feel better if you get it off your chest, Mitchell. We tried to be your friend. It took a lot of doing to make you see that what you were trying to accomplish didn't have to be done through violence." He looked resigned and then he sat down with his shoulder slumped forward. He was obviously ready to tell me what was bothering him.

"I've never said this to anyone and I don't want you to repeat it to any one." I nodded my head to give him the kind of courage to continue his story. "I never had a real family and unlike you, I didn't grow up with a mother and father to keep me safe. They were killed early on and then I was left alone to fend for myself. I know exactly what these kids are going through and I sympathize. I just don't know if I have what it takes to tell them what they want to hear. Kids of that young age are almost like lie detectors. If I'm not able to convince them, then it's on my head that they're going to be left behind."

"I don't think that you're telling me everything. You're leaving something out."

"Why can't you leave this the alone? Fine, I was in their same shoes, but then I was taken in to an orphanage. I learned to scrape and scratch for everything that I had. I stole, I tricked and I did what I had to do to survive. I don't want to be reminded of those times. I did some bad things back then. It was a matter of standing up on my own two feet. Those that ran the orphanage didn't really give a damn about any of us."

This was obviously keeping him from opening up to the *kinner*. I had to make him see that it was time to get past the past. It couldn't keep weighing him down and maybe since he had voiced his concerns, some of that trepidation about talking to *kinner* had vanished.

"You're going to have to find a way. What you did and how far you went to survive is none of my business. You did what you had to do. Do you really want to put these *kinner* through the same kind of hell that you went through? They could have a life. We could bring them back to the camp and give them parents that have their own *kinner* I even know a few young couples that will be interested in taking them in. I'm sorry that you didn't have that chance, but these *kinner* do have that chance and the only way that they're going to get it is by you giving your word. Tell them what they want to hear and maybe they will see to it that you're not the enemy."

"I really don't want to do this, Bethany, but it doesn't look like you're going to give me any other option. You're right, I don't want them to go through the same thing that I did. It would do my heart proud to know that they are with people that care for them and will treat them with nothing but kindness and love. A child of any age needs that kind of stability and without it they can turn to crime or something even more disastrous for the future." He was still hurting, but at least I made him see that the *kinner* should not suffer for those things that he had done when he was their age. "I'll talk to them, but I'm not going to promise anything.

"The one thing you have to know before you go in there is if you believe it…they will believe it. It's all in your delivery and how passionate you are on the subject." He was still shaking his head, like he couldn't believe that he had to do this, but the writing was on the wall.

Chapter 8

"I don't know how you convinced him, Bethany, but it's in all of our best interest if these kids come willingly and not have to be forced. We all know that kids can be loud when they want to be and we can't deal with that right now." Jacob was standing by the window, as the sun was just coming up over the horizon. We would have to do something about our water supply, because we were running low and these kids really did drink like fish. The one thing that they knew that they had to do was replenish the fluids in their bodies. They are still reluctant to eat. Maybe a kind word from Mitchell would go a long way.

"I didn't want to put Mitchell into that position, but the kids are quite strong willed. They want to hear it from the horse's mouth and they're not going to take anything less than complete honesty. His lie is going to have to be, so convincing that those *kinner* are never going to question it. If there's even a waiver in his voice, they will pounce on it and make him regret walking in there by himself. To that end, I think that we should make sure that everything is going OK."

"Mitchell's men are still on watch. They take turns doing that duty. I'm glad that we have him here with us, because without him and his men, I think that we would be run over without even knowing it was happening. At least with Mitchell's men looking out for us, there is a good chance that they will have a pretty good idea of what's coming before it actually arrives. I don't think we can stay here past today. We're risking getting caught and that might be OK for us and we could live with our choices, but we can't in good conscience allow these kids to fall into enemy hands."

"Jacob, you're right and we've seen what happens when *kinner* are corrupted. Mitchell became a soldier in his own right, but other kids younger than he is have turned to picking up a weapon. They were brainwashed into thinking that it was the only way. I guess recruiting kids is easier than trying to get an adult to pick up a weapon for their country. I don't like seeing *kinner* with guns in their hands. It makes me cringe to think what the future holds for them.

I followed Jacob and we stood outside the door "…
I was your age, maybe a little older, but I was
exactly where you are. Unfortunately, I didn't have
a good man like Jerome looking out for me or even
a good friend like Frankie to keep me from doing
anything ill advised. I lived hand and mouth,
scrounging for food on the streets and stealing from
anybody that got in my way. I would bring back
my bounty to those in charge of the orphanage and
they would take what I got. I wished that I could
tell you that things were going to get better, but if
you stay here they are never going to. I think you
all know that we could force you, but we'd rather
you come quietly and voluntarily."

"I'm sorry that you had to go through that and we
certainly don't want to go down that same road."

"I don't want your sympathy for what I did. I did
what I had to do at the time. I regret a lot of things.
What I'm doing now is making up for the sins that
I perpetrated on others over the years. By saving
you and giving you a life, I am saving myself and
washing away the scars on my soul. If that doesn't
convince you that I'm on the level, then maybe this
will." He reached in underneath his shirt and pulled

out the cross and laid it bare on the dirt floor in front of them. "I find strength in this and in the word of God. He's always with me in my heart and in my head. I'm going to give you this cross as a symbol of my trust in you. You can't keep it; you're only borrowing it, until after we get you safely away from here."

I saw the little girl reaching out with shaking hands. She was staring at Mitchell the entire time like she thought that he was going to snatch it away from her before she got her hands on it. She grabbed it, held it up to the light that was shining through a window. The sunlight bounced off the silver surface and shimmered like a beacon of light for others to follow.

"I really don't know what to say. I guess if you're willing to part with something like this, even for a little while, we can at least come with you. We want the life that you speak of and we don't want to scrounge for food. We are not built like Frankie and we need somebody to care for us. He took it upon himself to act as our guardian, although I don't think that he really wanted that kind of responsibility. Unfortunately, it was pushed upon him and he didn't have the heart to walk away from us. He said that he would be back and we believe him."

"You trust your friend and you should, but anything can happen to him while he's out there. These woods are dangerous. One wrong move and he could tumble down over an incline or be bitten by a poisonous spider or other wildlife. We will leave him a note with an explanation of what has happened. If he is as good as a survivor as I was, he will find his way to get back to you at the camp."

"Do you promise to leave your guns behind? We need to see that for ourselves and nothing is going to make us believe it, unless there is proof."

"I promise on that cross that we will lay down our arms. If that doesn't convince you, then I don't know what will. I'll even give you the benefit of the doubt and let you see the weapons before we leave here later today. We're going to try to move out when the sun is down. We're going to use the cover of darkness to use the paths that I have used in the past. I think I have stayed here long enough and I do have to get back to what I was doing." I'd heard what Mitchell had said and it certainly did make me see him in a different light.

He was obviously damaged; someone that had seen and done things that would probably make people from back home look at him like some kind of monster. I saw a little boy trying to be a man and showing some remarkable resolve in the face of overwhelming odds.

He stopped outside the door and looked at me "I hope that you're happy, because that brought back a lot of painful memories. I just hope that it was worth it and that it gets the desired results. I did tell you that these kids are not easily swayed. They want assurances and I'm going to have to do my best to give them that. I don't like to leave behind any weapon, but it's a small price to pay to get their cooperation."

Chapter 9

"I did what I could and it's up to you to take it the rest of the way, Bethany. You may not think that they trust you, but I think that you are the only one that they will trust. You have this mother quality that shines through. I think that if anybody was going to lead them, it would be you." This was high praise coming from a leader such as Mitchell and I had to believe that he was telling me the truth and not just throwing me to the wolves. He really did believe that I could give them that second chance at a life that they probably would never have without us or Mitchell getting involved.

"I think that you are a real hero and you may not believe that, but trust me…you are."

"It brings to mind an old television show that I saw one time. Do you know what a hero is?" I shook my head, because I didn't own a television and I had no idea what he was talking about. "A hero is somebody that is just too tired and too hungry to give a damn. I'm that tired and I don't give a damn.

I've known for quite some time that I had leadership thrust upon me. I didn't want it, I didn't seek it out and I certainly didn't ask anybody to follow me. It just sort of happened and I have to live with the responsibility of their lives each and every day." I could see that the death of Carl affected him, but he had a hard shell. There was nothing that was going to break through that tough exterior.

"I understand, my wife Bethany and I really do appreciate that you didn't go through with your plan. I'm just glad that we are able to look towards the future. I told you once that I would never forget and that is something that will never happen. I do forgive you for what you tried to do to me. I hope that eases the burden on your heart. I would never want to be the cause of you second guessing yourself. Carl showed exactly what is needed to make a difference in this world, but he also knew that you were the man and he tried to protect you with his life."

"I never asked him to." He walked away, leaving me and Jacob to deal with the *kinner*. We didn't have a whole lot of time and Mitchell wanted to get on the road right after we were packed and ready to go.

"Jacob, he's not an easy man to talk to. It took a lot for him to even go in there and talk to them. I saw vulnerability, but he sees that as a weakness and he tries to hide his good nature. I think he does it, so that he has the strength to show his men there is another way."

"I didn't realize that he was carrying so much and it must be very hard for him to lug around all of that mental luggage without snapping in half. I think looking back; we can consider ourselves lucky that we grew up relatively normal. We may not have had the technological advances that others did, but we were happy, healthy and had parents that truly loved us. He didn't have that and he decided that the only way was to look out after himself."

"I think that he would've been quite content with doing just that, but then El Diablo came into his life. He saw the way that his constant interference in his community was making people look like they were zombies and just going through the motions.

He decided to do something about it, having no idea what kind of revolution he had started. His actions speak louder than words, but his words hold a lot of weight with a lot of people. He uses his natural charisma and strength to make people see him as a viable option to getting their lives back."

"I think that I'm going to go down to the stream with Mitchell. I think that you should join me after you are finished with helping them pack up what little they have." I could use a dip into the cool waters, but to take my clothes off in front of mixed company was not the Amish way. I could cool myself off with throwing water into my face and that was exactly my idea.

"Just give me a little bit of time to prepare them and then I will come back out and we can go together." He nodded his head and then he went back towards the front door where Mitchell was now standing guard. He was disciplined. I don't think he had slept the entire time that we were here. You could see that he was on high alert. Any time that he did lay down, he just stared at the ceiling for hours on end.

I went in and this time they didn't cringe away like frighten little rabbits at the presence of the big bad wolf. "I don't even know your name."

"My name is Emmanuelle. But most people call me Emma for short. My friends are Stefan, Jules, Agatha and Jean. We grew up with Jerome and I don't think we've ever been apart in at least five years. Jerome and Frankie were the only ones that gave a damn about us. We trusted them and now they have abandoned us. We are grateful that you came along." She was their spokesperson and was helping them understand what was going on.

Emma was older than all of them, not by much, but enough to have the responsibility of their lives on her shoulders. "My name is Bethany, but I'm sure that you've heard it bandied about over the last day and a half. We have to go down to the stream to retrieve water and fill up the jugs that we have. When we return, we'll be leaving shortly. I see that you have everything ready." It almost pained me to realize just how little they had. Each one was holding a prize possession. Whether it was a piece of a stick or blanket or some kind of broke doll. It was just, so sad to see that their lives had come to this.

I was glad that the story that Mitchell had told them had gotten them to see that he could be trusted. I didn't like lying to them, but it was necessary for them to see that we were not the bad guys. Once we had gathered them up, we would show them that their fears were baseless. Jacob was waiting for me and I stepped lively, because I knew that time was of the essence.

"Those kids are remarkable and they have a resiliency the goes beyond anything that I would have at their age. I think of my *dochtah* and I know for certain that she would be able to survive. I just don't want to have to see her have to do something like that. It hurts me to know that they never had a true childhood. I guess I felt the same thing with those in the camp, but at least they had somebody that loved them. They have nothing, but themselves and Frankie, who abandoned them and left them. Just because he didn't like us, didn't mean that he had to run away."

"Bethany, you have to see it from his point of view. We were taking away his power, even if it was only borrowed from the death of a man that they cherished more than life itself. He wants to be the one to give them everything they need. When we came along, we ruined all of that. I'm just happy that somebody was able to talk them into coming." Jacob was standing at the door with two jugs in his hand. He handed me one of the empty. We went out to meet up with Mitchell and one of his men, who had decided to come along to carry the weight of these jugs after they were filled.

Chapter 10

The water against my face was jarring, but necessary to bring me back to reality. We may have had a plan, but it wasn't going to be easy by any means.

The sun had gone down and we didn't realize that the trek to the stream would be this long. It was made harder by the overgrown path they had to be cut down with a machete that Mitchell was using to do the task.

I finished washing up, feeling slightly more refreshed. I turned to see that Mitchell, Jacob and his man was standing there waiting for me. "I'm sorry, I didn't mean to take so long, but you have no idea what freshwater feels like fresh from the stream. It's like God is giving you a moment of reprieve and I was definitely well going to take it."

With that sentence Jacob smiled and said "I told them the same thing. They finally believed me when they did the same thing that you did. But we really do need to get going, because Mitchell has told me that the path back to our camp is not going to be an easy one. There are many obstacles, including a mountain that is going to have to be traversed. I didn't want to ask them how we're going to do that, because I really don't want to know."

It was harder to see going back than it was coming here. The sun had all but disappeared. I suddenly heard something in the distance. It made me stop and grab the shoulder of Jacob for some kind of support. The voices sounded raised and then there was somebody that had a smaller voice.

Mitchell indicated for us to be quiet. We snuck up and looked through the underbrush to see that El Diablo's men had found the orphanage. They even had two of Mitchell's men handcuffed and kneeling on the ground. I couldn't understand how this could've happened. I thought that we had a little bit more time before they would get here. Then it all became clear, when I looked and saw that Frankie was standing with the leader of the pack.

"I would say that Frankie didn't exactly run away. He thought it was a good idea to bring these men back to deal with us personally. I wonder if he knows what kind of mistake he has made." They were walking towards the orphanage where the kids were currently waiting for us to return. The leader stepped behind the two of Mitchell's men with a gun in hand. They were going to be executed

Rachel H. Kester

BOOK 7

Chapter 1

I looked at Jacob and Mitchell and I knew that they were both thinking about doing something. I understood the sentiment, because two men were going to lose their lives. They didn't do anything, but protecting Mitchell and giving their people a chance at a new life.

"I know what both of you are thinking and I implore that you don't do anything rash or reckless. We need to think this through and maybe we can talk to them and come to a reasonable solution. I'm sure that they can be reasoned with and we just need to find some way to reach them." I was tempted to take out the Bible, but I didn't think that this was the place or the time.

"I really do understand what you're saying, Bethany, but I don't think that I can just stand here and do nothing. Even your husband looks ready to fight and I could use all the help that I can get." The *mann* that had come down to fetch the water with us was now unstrapping his gun and holding it to his side.

"Mitchell, just give me the word and I'll take them out with extreme prejudice."

"I don't think that's a good idea. There are *kinner* in that building. If a stray bullet was to hit one of them, I don't think any one of us could live with ourselves." That brought to mind my *dochtah* Rebekah. As a protective *maemm*, I couldn't in good conscience allow them to just do something that might get one of them killed. Fighting fire with fire was not the answer, or at least it wasn't in my opinion.

"Unless you have any other bright ideas, Bethany, I think that I'm going to have to use force, whether I want to or not." Mitchell was at least thinking about an alternative solution. That was a far cry from the *mann* that I used to know. He was always ready with the gun, but knowing us had changed him to think of others first. He was one that finally convinced the kids to trust us. His story of his youth put a lot of things into perspective and gave me new insight into the *mann*.

"Bethany, I know that you don't want me to do this, but if I don't, then people are going to get killed. I don't think that I can have that on my conscience." To that end, Mitchell passed my husband a gun and showed him how to use it.

"All you have to do is take off the safety…aim and fire. It's pretty easy." To me, death was never that easy. I didn't want anybody to get killed, and I certainly didn't want to have my husband bear arms. It went against everything we believed in. We were the ones that turned the other cheek and if we didn't do that, then we wouldn't be a good example to others.

"I understand the trepidation about using a weapon, but sometimes it's unavoidable. I normally would just take them out with as many shots as it took. I think you might be rubbing off on me and I'm not sure that's a good thing or bad thing. I've even started to look towards the Bible for answers. There's a passage about turning the other cheek. I suppose you live by that motto every day. I don't know how you do that in a land that has been decimated by a natural catastrophe. People are always on edge and you can see that this kind of thing can bring the bad out of anybody."

"They haven't shot them yet and I can only assume that they are trying to get information out of them first. That at least gives us a moment to think of a better plan than going in there with guns blazing." I lifted my skirt, because it was dragging on the ground. I hugged my husband to me, knowing full well that he was starting to see Mitchell's point of view. I didn't like it, but I had to admire that my husband was not just going to stand on the sidelines and do nothing. Good men were going to die and I don't think that talking was going to get through to them.

"I know that you're going to do what you need to do, Mitchell. I would ask that you don't get my husband involved."

He wasn't even looking at me. He was staring at his men who were now kneeling on the ground with their hands over their heads. "I'm afraid that my coming into your life has made you both a part of this and for that I do apologize. Unfortunately, I will not try to convince your husband to stand down. I won't ask him to do anything that he doesn't feel comfortable with." It didn't look like it was going to take much convincing. My husband may have been holding my hand with one hand, but his other hand was now bunched up into a fist.

They were about to do something, but then we heard a commotion. We looked over to see that the guards were trying to shield their faces from rocks that were being thrown from inside the building. Kids being kids had decided to take matters into their own hands. I had to give them credit for standing up, but rocks were never going to be enough to conquer the enemy.

Jacob, Mitchell and his man Anderson looked at each other and then they made a decision on the fly. They came out guns blazing, catching the guards off guard. They were, so caught up in trying to protect themselves from rocks that they didn't even put up much of a fight. They turned and faced Mitchell and my husband. They were about to go for their gun, but they thought better of it. There was only one *mann* standing that didn't seem to be wavering. He wasn't going to go down without some sort of fight.

Chapter 2

"My name is Manuel and what you're doing here is only going to make you an enemy of my boss. I would suggest that you stand down." It looked to me like he was a beaten *mann*, but I didn't think that he was going to give up so easily. "You've gotten involved in something that you shouldn't. You should be scared out of your minds, because once my boss feels that you're a threat; there is no place that you can hide." His gun was lowered, but he was still holding onto it. That was making Mitchell very nervous and willing to put one into his head for his troubles.

"Before anybody else does anything, I want to say something. You may think that we are your enemy, but we're not. We're just trying to do the right thing. I'm not even sure that you know what that is and if you do, you're certainly not doing it. You threaten *kinner*, use them for your own advantage and that makes you feel good. You should be ashamed of yourselves. You're not men. You are animals, but I still believe that there is hope for you. Turn to your Bible and you'll learn that life doesn't have to have violence. There can be peace, just as long as everybody is willing to lay down their arms and help each other." It sounded good to me, but I did see the expression on Manuel's face. I knew that I was barking up the wrong tree.

"Young lady, you can't be serious. You're spouting the Bible to me of all people. I really don't think that you have any idea how over your head all of you really are. Mitchell is the only one that I respect, albeit only a little bit. He is very ill equipped to deal with what is coming and I just want you to know that I'm going to be there when my boss puts you all down for good." He was arrogant, full of himself, but he still was not relinquishing his hold on his weapon.

"That is no way to talk to my wife. If you're not respectful, then I might have to do something about it. You must know that you're beaten. Your men are not going to come to your rescue. You're holding onto that gun like it is a lifeline. It's a hindrance. You need to let it go. If you don't, then one of Mitchell's men might accidentally shoot you. My wife is right and you're not a *mann*. If you

124

were a real *mann*, you would put down the gun and settle your differences with words, instead of actions."

"You may be saying that, but I don't believe a word that's coming from your mouth, Jacob. You may be surprised to know that I know both you and Bethany. Let's just say that Frankie was very forthcoming about your names and where you came from. He overheard that you were Amish. It almost made me burst out laughing at the absurdity that you would actually consider going to war. Your people are supposed to be peace loving, strict in their moral code and yet here you are with a man that tends to hurt my boss. I might consider letting you walk away from this, but you're going to have to do it sooner rather than later."

"Put down the gun." He dropped the weapon. It landed onto the ground with a heavy thud. It was getting very dark and the only illumination that was coming from anywhere was the headlights of these vehicles. I could see something inside one of the trucks. I couldn't verify anything from my vantage point. His men were being cordial and weren't trying to be any kind of a nuisance. Manuel was another matter altogether and I could see that he was just looking for an opportunity to strike.

It came when Jacob went to retrieve his gun at his feet. I watched in horror, as he grabbed Jacob and produced a knife. He placed it up against his neck.

"This has never been his fight, Manuel. This is between your boss and me." Mitchell was trying to defuse the situation. It didn't look like he was going to listen to anything that he had to say.

"I don't care and I'm going to take him with me as insurance." He was about to do exactly that. Jacob looked at me and I began to shake my head vehemently. He didn't pay attention and soon he had that man's hand in his own. He was forcefully pulling that knife away from his neck. Manuel was a bit shocked. He tried to take back the reins of control, but it was in vain.

Jacob turned around with the knife now hung high in the air. They were struggling to find out who was going to get control of it. I waited with my heart almost leaping from my chest. That knife teetered from one side to the other, until Jacob slammed his hand up against the hood of one of the vehicles. He did that two times. Manuel did not scream in pain, but he did have to let go. The knife rolled down the hood and fell onto the ground with the blade sticking into the ground.

Jacob looked angry. I saw him begin to pummel the *mann*. He hit him in the stomach to blow the wind out of him. When he was doubled over, he struck against his nose. He stumbled backward, but Manuel wasn't going to go down without getting a few licks in himself. He leveled a right cross to my husband's jaw. It didn't even slow him down. Jacob was built like an ox and he stood his ground and swung his own fist against the side of Manuel's head. This staggered him and he looked like he was having a problem standing on his feet.

"My God, what are they feeding you in that Amish community of yours." He tried to tackle my husband. He was met with a brick wall. Jacob grabbed him by his hair. He pulled him up, so that he could punch him square in the mouth. One tooth became dislodged from Manuel's mouth. It fell lazily to the ground with blood spilling from the open wound. He fell backwards on his ass. Jacob was about to go after a defenseless man.

I went to him and put my hand on his shoulder. He looked at me with a glaring expression, until he realized who it was. He softened slightly. I could still see the blood on his knuckles and the way that he was looking at Manuel like he wanted to kill him.

"That's enough." My soothing words gave me back the husband that I knew and loved. He was still angry, but at least he was controlling it in a better way.

Chapter 3

"I want the kids secured, but it doesn't look like we have to worry about that." I followed Mitchell's gaze and they had now surrounded Frankie from all sides to make sure that he wasn't getting away. They were all holding rocks and he was now cowering in the circle that they had formed around him.

"I did this for all of you. Don't you understand that they only bring death and destruction with them? If we give them up, we can walk away from this." They weren't listening and apparently what Mitchell had said to them had really gotten through to them. They wanted the life that they had heard him speak of. They wanted to go back to the camp and be welcomed with open arms. It was that hope that they were feeding on. They weren't even going to allow their one true protector to stand in their way.

"I don't think that you did this out of malice, Frankie, but you have to see that you joining with them was wrong. They are cutting a swatch of destruction across your land and you allow it because you are too terrified to do anything about it. At least, Mitchell is doing something. I may not agree with his methods, but he does think before he acts. You are a child and you should be home sleeping in your own bed. I feel sorry for you, but rest assured, this is not going to stop me from helping you. Your friends, especially Emma wants to live without violence. They all want to have a life outside of this place. You can have that too, but you're going to have to get past this notion that the bad guys always win."

"I can't believe that you would still consider helping me. I brought them to your door and anybody else would have fed me to the wolves. I guess I might've been wrong about you, but you had to see it from my point of view. You came into our building with guns and then I overheard that you were being hunted by El Diablo. My friends would fall victim to a skirmish between the two of you. I only did what I thought was right. I think that even you could understand that."

"My husband will not agree with me, but I intend to take you with us. All of you are going to find that freedom. You won't have to make those kinds of decisions ever again."

"Hello." At the sound of a frail voice, we all turned and peered into one of the SUV's. There was somebody there. The voice was feminine, but that didn't mean that she wasn't a threat. Mitchell's men pulled their guns and surrounded the vehicle. They pointed at the poor woman in the back seat. She was obscured by the tinted. The door opened and there was a collective sigh of relief.

Inside was a woman with bandages over her eyes. She couldn't see a thing and was now cringing away from the feeling of the cool air coming into the vehicle. "Whose there? Please don't hurt me. I'll tell you anything you want to know." Mitchell looked around at his men and then over at me and I knew that he was asking me to intervene. Out of all of us, I was the best at keeping people calm. I was that soothing influence and Mitchell was not above using me in that regard.

I stepped over to the vehicle, feeling the crunch of the dirt underneath my feet. I climbed in beside her. I reached for her hand. She slapped it away. "I'm here to help. You're going to have to trust someone. I can't make that decision for you. You're either going to have to believe that we're not your enemy, or you continue to lash out for no good reason. I see that you are religious." I could see that she was holding the cross in your hand. The clasp was broken, but that didn't stop her from gripping it in a death like vise.

"I don't know who I can trust. The one man that I thought that I could turned out to be not who I thought he was. I really believed that he was kind and gentle, but then he came to my room last night with a knife." I didn't like how this was sounding, but I had to let her tell me in her own time. She began to weep uncontrollably, falling into my arms and me holding her.

"It's OK and you're with friends. I think that we should get you out of here. Maybe take a walk and feel the fresh air on your face."

"Get away from her, or you will be sorry." Manuel was panicking. I could see the desperation on its face. He tried to get up, but he was met with a swift kick in the ribs for even giving it an effort. "I mean it, she has nothing to do with this and I would suggest that you leave her the hell alone." There was obviously a connection between the two of them, but what that was, was their secret to tell.

"I don't think you get it, Manuel. I'm the one that's holding the gun. Remember that before you start spouting off for no good reason. She's obviously injured and I can see that she means a lot to you. I could use that and threaten her with bodily harm to get you to cooperate, but that is not the kind of man that I am anymore. Sometimes I think that I should go back to what I know, but I feel all of this regret for what I've done already."

"That's where you and I differ, Mitchell. I have no regrets. I would do everything all over again. My loyalty to my boss is never ending. I will fight to the death to protect him, but I don't think you know what that kind of loyalty is like." I could see the faraway look in Mitchell's eyes. I knew that he was thinking about his friend, who had shown his loyalty with the bravery that came from his own demise.

Chapter 4

Mitchell corralled all the men into the building and tied them up. He was going to leave them for El Diablo to find and deal with personally. It was a fate worse than death, but I was a small voice in a din of people that were not going to listen.

"Mitchell, you can't do this and you just finished saying that you weren't the same *mann*. Was that all just words or are you going to prove it? This may have been what you would do in the past, but this is another chapter of your life. You can't just walk away and leave them to fend for themselves. At the very least, you should loosen their bonds. Give them the possibility of escape. I would even suggest leaving them some rations, but I don't think that you're going to do that."

"Bethany, you're the voice of my conscience and sometimes I just wish that you would get out of my head. You're right and I'm wrong, but that isn't going to be the first time and it's not going to be the last. If you want to be heard, then you're going to have to raise your voice metaphorically speaking. I understand what you're saying and I will have the bonds loosened. You've also given me a good idea. I don't think it's a good idea that I should leave Manuel. I'm going to take him as leverage. I get this feeling like his connection to El Diablo is a lot more personal than he lets on. I see it in the way that he talks. I get a pretty good idea that El Diablo may think twice about attacking us if he is with us."

"What about the girl? You can't possibly think that you can leave her in her condition out here in the middle of nowhere. It wouldn't be right and I think you know that." I wanted him to see that this woman needed our help. I could see the resignation on his face.

"OK, we'll take the girl with us and I'll even do you one better. My man Nicholas has some medical training. He went to university for four years in the States. He only returned recently at my bequest. He's doing his internship and will be a doctor in about six months. I felt kind of bad for taking him away from his studies, but this was more important than just one person." He called over Nicholas and he went over to the woman, but the woman shied away from him. She would only trust my voice. I was going to have to pave the way for her to be looked after.

"We can't stay here for very much longer, Bethany. Do what you can to sooth her nerves, but then we're really going to have to get on the road as soon as possible. We're going to take their vehicles. The windows are tinted, so his men may not know right away that we have commandeered them. It would give us a fighting chance. We might be able to go further than we ever could before." I liked that idea, but I was going to have to convince the woman.

"My name is Bethany. You've already met me, but I have not had the pleasure."

"It's Gabrielle." It was all that she was going to say for the moment. I could see that there was something weighing heavily on her mind.

"Do you start to tell me what happened to you? Do you feel strong enough to continue?"

"Like I said, he bought a knife into my bedroom. I thought that he was joking, but then I saw the seriousness in his face. He had two of his men hold me down. While I was thrashing, he was stabbing at my eyes. He finally got frustrated and left me to bleed. It was just a good thing that one of his maids had decided to help me. She bandaged my eyes. My brother came and told me that I had to go with him. I knew that he was trying to protect me. El Diablo would be back to finish the job. When he gets frustrated, he can overthink things. He has to go and compose himself."

It finally dawned on me that she was the only person that had seen El Diablo's face. Each and every time, he wore a mask of a skeleton on his face. This was the reason why he was nicknamed El Diablo. He surrounded himself in death. He looked like death in the mask. He had no problems using that to terrify the locals.

"I'm blind and I know that. I've accepted that, but I really don't want to live. I need you to put me out of my misery. I know that it's a hard thing to ask of you, but I trust you more than anybody. You are kind and I would hope that you would see that this is the only way." I understood why she felt that way, but there was no way that I could take away her pain in the way that she requested. I did struggle with the idea of someone that was suffering, but she seemed stronger than she was letting on. I wanted to give her a chance and instead of putting a gun to her head, I placed a Bible in her hands. The tears that were falling suddenly stopped. She grabbed it with the cross still embedded in the palm of her left hand.

Chapter 5

"I want you to really think about this, Gabrielle. I really don't think you want to die. You must know that people live with blindness. You can do the same thing and it just means that you're going to have to *schaffe* harder than you've ever had to *schaffe* in your life. You'll have to fight and keep fighting, until you don't have anything left inside of you."

"*Schaffe*...what is that? I explained to her that it meant work.

"You don't understand. I'm already dead. I might be blind and I might want to die, but I'm not the only one that wants to get rid of me. Hanson — and I don't even know if that's his real name —will want to finish the job. He won't care how it's done. Just as long as there's proof that my head is on a stake somewhere. You must have already realized that I have seen his face. There's only a few in his inner circle that has been allowed to do that. I guess he thought that he was through with me. By that same token, he believed that I could be a detriment to his organization." I could see a new life on her face. Her teeth were grinding like she really didn't want to die.

"Like I said, you're going to have to fight. The best way to do that is to stay with us and give a face to the devil itself. If you can do that, then we can bring him to justice. All we really need for you to do is verify his voice. We can take it the rest of the way." I was still holding her hand, lovingly squeezing it and showing her that she was not alone in this world.

"I don't know and I should talk to my brother before I make any sort of decisions. He's the only one that has had my back. He thought it was a bad idea for me to get involved with Hanson. He wasn't even allowed to see the man underneath the mask. I felt sort of special that he would allow me. I guess I shouldn't feel that way, because having that knowledge has only made me a target."

"I don't know who your *bruder* is, but I don't think that he would want you to end it all." One of these men was her *bruder* and I had a pretty good idea of who it might be. He was quite adamant that we don't touch her. It stood to reason that Manuel was her *bruder* "Is Manuel your *bruder*?" At the sound of his name, she lit up like the 4th of July.

"Yes, I want to see him or at least talk to him. I suppose it's good that I have a sense of humor, because without it, I would probably kill myself. I don't see how I could do that with no eyesight, but I would try to find a way." I had no doubt that her first intention was to do that. Nicholas was waiting. I had to tell her that it was in her best interest to allow him to take a look.

"I will allow somebody to look at me, but only if you are there the entire time. You need to promise me that you'll be there, Bethany. You're the only one that has shown me any kind of kindness. I can feel a wave of pity coming from everybody else. I don't feel that from you or maybe it's mixed with compassion, I just don't know." I motioned for Nicholas to come forward. He went around to the other side and sat beside her.

"I'm just going to take these off and have a look at what I'm dealing with. When I do take them off, I need you to tell me if you can see anything." He unwrapped the bandages slowly, lifted them from her eyes and I could see the damage that was done. In his overzealous way, Hanson had probably done something right. Some of the strikes were against the side of her eye and she must've been moving at the time. She did tell me that she was thrashing back and forth. That would stop him from getting a pinpoint accuracy.

"I have some good news and I have some bad news. The good news is that you're not going to be blind. The bad news is that you won't have 20/20 vision. One of your eyes might be damaged beyond repair, but the other one seems to have taken the brunt of the attack and survived. I'm going to need to get some medication to prevent infection. I think that you're not as bad off, as you might have thought."

"I can see shapes in one eye and colors in the other. I guess things could be worse." I helped her to walk around. She seemed to be able to discern some things around her. Manuel was watching intently, shaking his head and trying his best not to announce the fact that she was his sister. There was no way that I could say anything to Mitchell or Jacob for that matter. They might want to use her against Manuel. It was a good tactic, but not something that I would condone. I had to make a hard decision. I was going to keep this from both Jacob and Mitchell. It hurt me to do so, but I didn't see any other way around it.

Chapter 6

"I hear from Nicholas that she's not as bad off as she appeared. That's good news. I know for fact that she is the only one that has seen El Diablo's face. She may know him as Hanson, but that is probably not his real name. I think he hides underneath that mask for a reason. He really doesn't want anybody to know just what kind of despicable monster he is. It means that he has something to hide and I intend to uncover it and shine the light of day in his eyes." Mitchell was already gathering the troops and it wasn't going to be long before we were going to hit the road.

"I don't like this, Mitchell. I want to go on the record to say that this is a very bad idea. You think that this El Diablo character is going to care that we have her in our possession? You think that that he's going to care that Manuel has been taken hostage? We've already learned that he really doesn't think like anybody else. His main concern is complete dominance over everything in his wake. He doesn't want any loose ends. If he considers Manuel to be a weakness, then he will surely allow us to kill him just for spite."

"Bethany makes a valid point, Mitchell. My wife may not be on board with your tactics, but she speaks the truth. I'm glad that she's in my life, because I don't think that otherwise I could be the man that she wants me to be. In this unforgiving environment, I almost lost it and I hurt somebody severely with my bare hands. I don't think I would've stopped. She touched my shoulder and brought me back to reality. Like you said, she is the conscience of the group. We're going to have to pay attention to her. I know that I will, but what you do is going to be your decision, Mitchell."

I went over to Gabrielle, who was sitting on the ground with Nicholas by her side. He was using a flashlight to make a better determination on her condition.

"Your left eye is swollen, but I believe in time that will diminish. When that does happen, you'll be able to see out of that eye. Unfortunately, the other one that you say that you can see colors is just phantom colors. It's your other eye trying to compensate for losing the sight from the other. I don't know how quite to tell you this, but this one eye is most likely going to be completely blind. I know this is not what you wanted to hear, Gabrielle. I'm just trying to help you to deal with what you're going to have to go through. A person with one eye can lose a lot of equilibrium. It's going to take a lot for you to adjust."

"I want to talk to my brother....I want to talk to my brother...I want to talk to my brother." I could see that she was getting unhinged. She was going to do something that would ruin everything. I sat down and held her hand in both of mine.

I whispered into her ear, so that Nicholas couldn't hear a word that I was saying. "It's OK, Gabrielle. Your *bruder* is coming with us. You can't let on. They don't know your connection and I would rather keep it that way. I think that you would want that to, or maybe I have been mistaken about your bond. Just nod your head to confirm to me that you are going to keep your mouth shut." I waited with bated breath, but finally she did relent. She was nodding her head, but she didn't like it. She now knew that her *bruder* was going to be by her side.

We gathered together and we all looked at the orphanage one last time. It had become somewhat of a surrogate home. I could walk away with the knowledge that I was making a real difference in people's lives. There was no second guessing and we drove away in those black SUV's. The *kinner* piled in the back. They were ducking down, so that there was no possibility that anybody would see them.

I think everybody was on edge, because nobody was saying anything. They were looking at those faces that they were driving by. Each one was trying to peer inside, but it was very difficult. They would have to place their hands directly on the glass to even perceive anything. It made me feel good that we could drive in relative obscurity. Everybody would think that we were the enemy. It was basically a Trojan horse and I read the story of how this tactic was used back in the day.

I was a very avid reader and even coming here had turned me on to other books that had me literally at a loss for words.

Gabrielle was sitting right beside me, holding my hand and keeping me as close as possible. I turned toward Frankie, but he had become withdrawn and was now looking out the window. He was still trying to figure out what the best thing to do was. I kind of worried that he was thinking about making a run for it again. I had to make him see that the life that he was leading was only going to end one way.

Chapter 7

I sidled up to Frankie and placed my hand on his knee in a reassuring way. "You're doing the right thing, Frankie. There's no point in trying to chastise yourself for something that was beyond your control. You finished telling me that you only did it to protect your friends. I think that was very admirable. Unfortunately, the way that you did it was only going to get all of you killed. What would've happened after they were finished with us? Would they really let you go, or would they try to force you into doing their bidding?"

"I just don't understand how they could possibly go against me like that. I saw the look in their eyes. If I had put up any kind of fight they would've smashed me to death with those rocks. I guess you really did get through to them. I suppose I should be grateful that somebody did. It might've been ill advised and I should have thought it through more, but I was just going on instinct." We were not avoiding the streets and we were staying on the main road. It put us in the limelight of anybody that we crossed paths with. They would believe that we were the enemy. It would be known to El Diablo that his men were still scouring the countryside for the ones that were making life difficult for him.

"I'm sorry, I guess I wasn't listening. I'm still worried about what we're going to do about all of this. Frankie, I doubt that you saw his face, but I get the feeling like you had a heart to heart with the man. Can you tell me what was said, or do you feel like you need to keep that to yourself. I'll respect you either way, but I think it would do your heart good to let it out. You've obviously been through a lot. I can't even begin to think about what you've seen in your life. I do want you to know that I would never hurt you or your friends. I just want to find you the happiness that you deserve."

"That's just it, Bethany. I don't know if I deserve the kind of happiness that you describe. I've been scrounging and fighting for everything all my life. I don't know anything better. I would like to, but I really don't know how I'm going to react with somebody trying to tell me what to do. I've been independent for some time and even our guardian knew from the moment that he met that I wasn't just going to bow down to his will. He allowed me to make my own decisions. I'm not sure if I'm going to enjoy having a tether around my neck." He had obviously given this some thought. It was my time to show him that he was on the right path.

"You say that you don't know a good thing when you see it, but maybe you just need somebody to guide you. I'll be glad to take you underneath my wing when get back to camp. I'll find you a family that will love you. I will not give up. If I can't do that for you, then I will take the responsibility onto myself." I was basically telling him that I would adopt him. I guess in retrospect, he really did feel like a little *bruder*. I could give him the guidance and structure that he was looking for. He probably didn't even know that he was looking for it.

He was silent for a moment and then he turned to me with questioning eyes. "I can't believe that you would even consider doing something like that. You're too good for these people. I cringe to think what would happen if they didn't have you along to be the voice of reason. I'll give you the benefit of the doubt, but how far that goes only time will tell." He went back to looking out the window. At

152

least I gave him an insight into the future that he could have. He didn't have to die on the streets like a dog, when a loving family was a real possibility.

"I heard what you said to him and I hope you mean it. I heard him talking to Hanson. I could sense something in his voice. He wanted to be confident and strong, but he's still a little boy. He might not project that. You have given him something to think about. That's more than anybody else has done in his life." Gabrielle was feeling a little better. She was trying her best to help me see that I was not just blowing smoke. I didn't want to give false promises, but I was not even sure if he were going to survive long enough to give these kids the future that they deserved. *Kinner* should be able to play safely outdoors, laugh with childish glee and not have to worry about where their next meal was coming from.

Sometimes I think that I have bitten off more than I can chew. If I didn't, then who would? Who would stand up for these *kinner* and give them a chance to live a normal life without fear of reprisal or being taken to become somebody's personal army? I would do that and I would be damned proud to call any one of these my *bobli*.

Chapter 8

Frankie was at least cognitive of what he had done. He had regrets, but he had only made those decisions out of necessity. His friends were in danger and he wanted to do something to protect them, even if it meant putting us into the line of fire of El Diablo. He had no problem doing that. He felt bad about it, but for the most part he was only doing it because he wanted to survive. He knew that El Diablo was not going to give up. If the kids got in the way, then they would be a casualty of that war. I had to admit, I admired the young man and I don't think that he made the decision to go against us lightly.

"What are you smiling about?" I could hear the tone in Mitchell's voice. I turned to see that Manuel was almost laughing in his face. "I don't particularly enjoy you looking at me like that." It made him seem like he knew something that we didn't and that was making Mitchell take that as a personal affront.

"You have no idea what kind of storm is coming your way. I'm going to be right there to see it up close and personal. I'll make sure that you're the last to go, Mitchell. Everybody else will die first. I'll make you watch, as I put a bullet into each of their heads. If I don't do that, then my boss will. It might give him a great satisfaction to put an end to this rebellion. Yes, I think that I would get great satisfaction out of seeing him do that." He really shouldn't have been pushing Mitchell. I would say that he was getting to that point where Mitchell was going to do something about it.

"I don't think you understand what's happening here, Manuel. You're my prisoner and you should be begging me for your life, but you're not. What you say might be true, but trust in the fact that we will not give up. It's not in our DNA and if you knew anything about the Haitian people, you would know that by now. You are an interloper, someone that shouldn't even be here. You probably only came here because this El Diablo decided to make his stand against people that weren't going to fight back. Unfortunately, those days have come and gone. They have someone that will stand up for

156

them." He began to snicker and Mitchell reeled back and punched him in the nose. The blood spilled and I tried to stop him. He looked to me and made me know beyond a shadow of a doubt that I shouldn't get involved.

"He's not a threat to you, Mitchell. He's just trying to push your buttons." I was going to have to try to stop him from becoming the monster that he thought he was. "You can't give in to him. He enjoys making you lose a part of yourself. You can see it in his eyes. He just wants to make you into a killer. We both know that you've left that life behind and you only go back when you absolutely have to." He looked to me for a second and then he continued the assault. He pulled out a knife and plunged it into this man's leg.

"IEEEEEEEEE." He screamed and then he shut his mouth and stared daggers into Mitchell's eyes.

"I don't hear you saying anything else, Manuel. Could it be, because you have something stuck in your leg? Let's see if we can't do something about the other one getting lonely." He plunged the knife again into his other leg. It was just good luck they didn't sever any arteries. Mitchell seemed to know exactly what he was doing, but I didn't like it.

"I'm begging you to lay off, Mitchell. He's just trying to goad you into doing something stupid. You can't let him get underneath your skin like that. He likes playing head games, manipulating you for his own purposes. Don't give in and he won't have any power over you." Amazingly, the wounds that he had inflicted weren't bleeding all that much. The knife that he had used was slim and had no real substance. I would say that it was meant to inflict pain. It had obviously done that and then some.

"I believe that you are right about him, Bethany. It's good that you are here, because I could've done some real damage. This is just something that is putting a smile on my face. I would never consciously kill him, because he's worth more to me alive than dead. I still don't know if El Diablo will back down because we have him. I think we're better off with him than without him." Manuel was still staring at him, begging him with his eyes to do something. Mitchell wasn't falling for this obvious attempt to kill him.

158

It was a good thing that Gabrielle didn't say anything. She was his sister and for her not to say anything at all during this obvious attempt to torture had to take an amazing willpower

Chapter 9

"Manuel, if there's anything that you want to say about your boss, then this is the time to do it. You can't possibly believe that your loyalty is going to get you anywhere. This is going to end one way and we both know it. I'm not naïve to think that I'm going to live to a ripe old age of eighty. I'll be lucky to live, until I am thirty with the way that I'm going. You can end this all right now and I'll be glad to put you out of your misery. Just tell me what I need to know about your boss and all this can be over with." It appeared that Mitchell's tactic had changed and now he was more interested in his boss.

"I would gladly tell you everything I know about my boss, except that I don't think that you will kill me. If I thought that you would, I would spill my guts and tell you everything I know. It's not much, but it's enough to give you a good understanding of what you're dealing with. My boss is not an easy person to live with and his temperament can get a little out of control. I see that you've noticed the scar on my cheek. That was courtesy of his hand and the huge ring that he wears. I think he only wears it to scare the locals. He hangs it around his neck, while he wears black gloves and that death mask to give him the air of somebody that was superhuman or even supernatural for that matter." Manuel was still trying one last time to get the upper hand. I had to admit that he was good at these games. If Mitchell had been a fool, he might've fell for his obvious attempt to get him to kill him.

Mitchell motioned for the driver to pull over and we were now out of the line of sight of the locals. There was a stream nearby and he had decided to allow everybody a moment of rest before moving on. I took Gabrielle's hand and I helped her out of the truck. We walked down to the river's edge with everybody. I could hear Mitchell still lambasting Manuel for his beliefs.

"Bethany, I would not underestimate my brother. If he really wants something, then there isn't anything that anybody's going to do to stop him. He may seem weak at the moment, but he's just waiting for the right time. You have to know that and you can't be foolish enough to think that he's just as powerless as any other hostage. He's always surveying and looking at his options. Sooner or later, he'll find a way to break free. That's when he's the most dangerous. I think it goes without saying that an animal when cornered will come out with its claws bared."

"I really don't think we have to worry about that, Gabrielle. Your *bruder* is in no position to do anything. He's surrounded by men and they're constantly keeping an eye on him. There's really no way that he can get away and I think we both know…" I didn't get a chance to say anything else. I heard somebody scream and turned to see that one of Mitchell's men was down. Gabrielle's *bruder* Manuel was behind him with a knife.

He sliced across the man's throat. The arterial spray landed on the ground with the life in the eyes diminishing quickly. Nicholas looked on in horror. I could see that he wanted to help, but there was no way to get close enough to do anything. Manuel was still holding the *mann* by the hair and glaring at Mitchell.

162

"I see that you're not going to allow us to get close enough to help him. I just need you to know that when he dies, then your life is worth nothing." He got a smirk for a response. Manuel was mocking Mitchell by saying nothing. He was letting this *mann* die in front of my eyes. The kids were beside themselves. They were cowering behind trees watching all of this play out in front of them. This was not something for their eyes to see. Unfortunately it was like an accident that you couldn't look away.

When the *mann* finally expired, Manuel dropped the man on the ground. He made a motion with his hand towards Mitchell to come get him. He didn't even try to run and Mitchell was on him in a second. They fell to the ground and Manuel fought valiantly, but Mitchell was determined. I saw the struggle end. Both men lay on top of each other and I had no idea who had gotten the best of the other. It wasn't until Mitchell stood up with blood on his shirt that we all knew the truth. We all looked to see that there was the knife inside Manuel's chest.

Nicholas was kneeling behind Mitchell and he was trying to get a pulse from the *mann* that had just lost his life. He looked despondent and was shaking his head back and forth like he couldn't believe that this actually happened. Jacob and I walked over with Gabrielle in tow. We all looked down at Manuel.

He was trying to say something. We got close enough and then that whisper of two words flowed into the air "Thank you". At those two words, Mitchell kicked him in the stomach and walked away with this anger showing on his face.

"He did that because he wanted to die. It's the only way out of this life. He got his wish and I hope to God he burns in hell." I wanted to tell him that every life was worth something, but I didn't think that he wanted to hear it at the moment. It stood to reason that he would feel that loss. He could see Manuel's eyes would be haunting him in his dreams. It was something that he was going to have to live with.

Chapter 10

Mitchell had blood on his clothes and Nicholas was the first one to come over and see if he was OK. He waved his hand. He didn't want to be bothered and it didn't matter if he was injured. I think that he would've taken that pain in response for the death that he had just caused another human being.

"Mitchell, you did what you had to. I may not think it was right, but what's done is done. You need to look to the future and Manuel is now just one of those casualties that you speak of in hushed tones. I know that Bethany wants to speak to you. I'm not sure if you want to hear what she has to say. It might be that you have done this before, but since we came into your life, things have changed dramatically. You don't just look to use violence, unless you are pushed beyond your limits." I could understand why Jacob was trying to get through to him. He looked like he was shocked by what he did in the spur of the moment.

He was staring out at the lake. His hands were bunched up into fists and blood dripping from them onto the ground. "You don't understand. I didn't want to kill him, but he left me no choice. That's not what's bothering me. What's bothering me is that I don't think this is ever going to end. I believe that one of these days, I will be the one on the receiving end of the knife. It's inevitable. I try to wrap my mind around the fact that I will burn in hell for the things that I've done."

"Mitchell, I want you to know that I can forgive what you did here. I know that it was unavoidable. You lost yourself in a moment of complete and unadulterated anger. He killed that *mann*. That is something that you couldn't turn the other cheek for. He knew that and he was banking on it. You still need to trust yourself. Use those tools that we gave you to look beyond the violence. These kids need you and we need you to be at your best. You can't do that with this hanging over your head. Come with me and we're going to sit and look at your options." He followed like he was in a trance with his hands bunched still to his side. He was

166

trying to deal with the fact that he killed another human.

I talked to him about the Bible. I gave him reassurances that God would forgive his trespasses. He just needed to confess to a priest.

"Bethany, I don't think it's right that I can be forgiven for my sins, just because I want to be. That to me is the coward's way out. I've never gone the easy way."

"Mitchell, it's never easy admitting that you were wrong. Every man or woman has the capacity to do heinous things. Murder is in everybody's heart, but we fight that urge to lash out each and every day. You've learned to do that yourself. If you think you haven't, then you really don't know what kind of man you are." He lowered his head and began to sob into my shoulder. I stroked his hair and let him get it all out.

His weakness was not shown to others and we were away from anybody that could see what was going on. "I just don't know what I'm going to do from one moment the next. I have this need to do the right thing, but I also don't know what that is sometimes. It makes me regret some of the things I've done. What you don't understand is that I don't want forgiveness for killing Manuel. I will gladly take whatever punishment God gives out. I just hope that I did something to lend a hand to Holden. He was the man that was killed. I need to go see his family and tell them that their daddy is not coming home anymore." He got up, dusted himself off and reached down to pull me to my feet.

"I'll be there with you and you can tell them that he died a hero."

"A hero or not, he is still dead and it was on my watch. I know the look that I'm going to get. I'm sure that a strike of a hand against my face is soon to come. His mother will look at me like I am the devil. This is something that I'll never be able to wipe away with just some soothing words." We walked back to the others and climbed back into the vehicles. I was sitting right beside Manuel's sister.

"I hope that you're happy with yourself, Bethany. My brother may have not been a good man, but he was my brother." I didn't have any words for her and we continued on our journey down the road and away from the death that was now permeating in the air. Holden was buried and in the last attempt to give dignity to the dead, Mitchell had also ordered that Manuel be buried alongside him. This was met with harsh words from his men. He was adamant and they followed his leadership to the letter.

"Bethany, I hope that you talked with Mitchell. His men need him to be ready for just about anything. The last they saw of him, he was a shell of himself. When he came back he looked like he was ready to continue what he had started." Jacob was sitting on the other side of me and he was holding my hand. I was glad to have him here with me during this troubling time. We should've been home with my *dochtah*, but unfortunately, circumstances dictated that we stay and fight a fight that we never really thought that we were going to have to.

"I told him what he needed here. I'm not sure if I even believed it, but I thought that it was best that he was able to stand up on his own two feet. If I told him exactly what I felt, then I don't think that he would've been able to look at me in the eyes. You know that I don't condone violence. What he did to that *mann* was wrong. It doesn't matter if Manuel killed his *mann*. That was no excuse for him to exact that type of vengeance. I know that he only did it in the name of Holden. It might've been done in self defense, but I think we both know that's not the case."

"Bethany, I know what you mean. He could've pulled his gun and made him drop the knife. Unfortunately, he felt honor bound to use his bare hands. Things look like they change and then they don't. It was an interesting way to see things and I guess we could only do so much.

"I would say that we are far from safe." I heard Mitchell's voice from up front. We craned our necks to see what was going on. The sight that reached our eyes was not something that was pleasant. Jeeps were sitting in front of the road and there was a man with a death mask standing with a bullhorn.

"I think we all know that you're not my men inside those vehicles. For you to hide yourself in plain sight makes you either brave or foolish. I suggest that you come out with your hands up and I might show mercy. By the way, my name is El Diablo. I do believe that you know me and have been trying to find me. I'm right here. It's time that you finally answer for your interference." We were surrounded, unable to do anything to fix what was wrong. If we tried to run, we would be gunned down. Our lives would be gone in an instant.

I looked towards Mitchell. He was holding onto the dashboard and it didn't look like he had any idea on what to do.

BOOK 8

Chapter 1

Mitchell looked like he was concentrating on something, but it was pretty much a mystery to me and Jacob. He was staring out at the *mann* known as El Diablo.

"I really don't think that we have much choice. We should just get it over with and hopefully he will listen and won't do anything rash." I was trying to get Mitchell's attention, but he didn't seem to be listening to me. Then he did something that was completely out of character. He smiled. It was weird seeing him do that and it sent this cold chill down my spine. His brow furrowed and his eyes focused. He turned to me and Jacob. I had a feeling I wasn't going to like what he was going to say next.

"I only told one other person what I was up to. Believe me; he wasn't all that happy with how I was going to conduct business." He leaned in and whispered to us what this was all about. Jacob and I looked at each other and couldn't believe that he could be this kind of evil genius. "I don't want you

174

to tell me that I'm doing something wrong, Bethany. We both know that what I do is for the good of my people and I would like some kind of support."

"I don't know how I can give you support when you tell us your plan and it sounds like a fool's errand. It's suicide and you're just asking for a bullet into the head." He was still looking straight ahead. He wasn't even wavering from what he was going to do. "Just listen to me. I'm sure that if we talk to El Diablo that we'll be able to come to some kind of reasonable solution." I knew that the words sounded stupid when I was saying them. Mitchell looked like he had made the decision and wasn't going to back down for anybody.

"I appreciate your counsel and I do want you to know that killing has never been easy for me. Destroying lives and making widows of wives, and mourning women of sisters is not my idea of a good time. It's just that I was thrust into this position and now I'm going to have to play the part that I was dealt. Like all of us, we have our own special thing that we can do the best and mine is leading men into battle. I thought that I would be an artist, but apparently I also had this magnetic personality that made people follow me into sticky situations."

I looked out the window and saw that El Diablo and his men were getting antsy. He had already given us strict orders to get out of our vehicles and put our hands over our heads.

"I don't think I can talk you out of this, but I do want to know that both Jacob and I are with you every step of the way." I didn't believe a word that I was saying, but I had to give him false hope. He needed somebody to stand by him. I feared that his men were not going to be exactly happy with his decision. He was going to give himself up, but that was just part of the plan. The rest of it was almost too hard for me to even grasp the concept. Things had to go exactly the right way or it would go sideways and there would be a lot of bloodshed, not unlike what happened to Gabrielle's *bruder*.

Come to think of her, she was still sitting there looking despondent and not able to look any of us in the eye. She probably thought that what happened was her fault. If it wasn't for her trying to

176

get away from El Diablo none of this unfortunate business would be happening. I wanted to console her, tell her that it wasn't her fault, but I didn't have time to get into this bit of business. She was just going to have to handle her guilty conscience on her own.

"I really do need you both to stay here and watch my back. Things are going to happen very quickly and if you blink, you're going to miss it. Trust that this will work, because it's the only way that we're going to finally be rid of this blight on humanity. El Diablo may be new to this area, but I doubt that this is his first time in a dictatorship kind of role. I would think that he would want to have everybody see his face. It appears that the wants to hide behind the myth or mask." I tried to reach for him, pull him back before he did anything that he was going to regret.

Jacob grabbed my hand and pulled me away from him. I looked to him to see that he was serious about letting Mitchell do this. "If we try to stop him, he'll just hate us. We need to give him moral support and to show him that we will follow him. It's the only way that he's going to have the strength and the courage to take the fight to El Diablo." I knew that Jacob was telling me the truth, but I just didn't want to hear it. I finally relented. I moved to the edge of my seat. I was able to see what was going on. He stepped out of the truck and I felt a cool breeze coming into the area. He stepped down the short distance to where El Diablo was now standing and waiting. He had his hands over his head. I knew that he was never going to surrender and that this was just a ploy to get close.

Chapter 2

It was like watching an old western. I've recently seen a video that was brought into camp that had me enjoying that genre of entertainment. It was kind of like our Amish background, where there was no electricity or modern technology to get in the way. It was just one man with a lone six shooter about to take on bandits that outnumbered him by 10-1. You'd think that they would have the upper hand, but the hero always found a way to turn things to his advantage.

"Jacob, he's a cowboy and he's going to get himself killed. His plan is ludicrous. If he does make it as close as he wants to, then he might just turn into a martyr. We don't want him to die and he's basically the glue that is holding all of us together. Without him, we would fall apart and there isn't anybody else that can fit into his shoes."

"I know what you're saying, Bethany, but he needs to do this. We can't dictate the rules of war. We may not like it, but this is war and he's more than capable of handling himself. He's already shown that on several occasions. I would take you back to what has happened to Gabrielle's *bruder*. There was a cold calculating feel to how he dealt with that particular situation. We both know that he's been trying to be a better man, but sometimes he needs to show his ruthlessness to get the respect of the men."

I had overheard some conversations that the men had. They were quite vocal about their response to what had happened to Gabrielle's *bruder*. Most of them said that it couldn't happen to a better guy, but there were a few like me that thought that he was going into a fight that was going to end with one of them dead at the other's hands.

"I don't want to sit here and do nothing. It makes me feel like I'm just a spectator. I want to do something, but I don't know what it is that I can do. I know that he thinks he's doing what is right, but it's only his pride getting in the way. His ego is telling him that he is invincible and we both know how frail the human body really is." I always thought that my *daett* was a hero and nothing could happen to him. It wasn't until his first heart attack that I found out that he was just as human as anybody else. I think that was the first time that I lost a bit of my childhood.

"I feel the same way that you do, Bethany. I think you know that he's been rubbing off on me a little bit. I guess I lost control and I can still feel the swelling of my fist from what I did. I'm not proud of it and I know that you looked at me like you didn't know me anymore. I do apologize for that, but sometimes I forget that I'm supposed to turn the other cheek."

I felt a hand touch me. Gabrielle was still looking out the window, but now had reached out for some kind of human contact. I held her and I heard her take a breath when she found comfort in my fingers touching hers.

"Jacob, what I saw in you was a *mann* that wanted to do something. What I saw in you was a *mann* that was willing to do practically anything and that scared me. I always considered you a person that wouldn't be caught dead laying a hand on anybody. When I saw you go a bit crazy, it concerned me that you wouldn't be able to pull yourself back. I don't want you to have blood on your hands. I know that being pacifists might not be the right kind of help for Mitchell."

"That's just it, Bethany, I think us being here has shown him that he doesn't always have to resort to physicality. He can use his God given wits and I've seen him walk away from the easy way. His plan for taking hostages was not a new one. He was just using a tried and true method that had been perpetrated on others. He wanted to help his people, but now he knows that he can't just sit on his hands. He has to fight back and we're going to have to learn to roll with the punches."

He was walking slowly towards El Diablo's men, his hand over his head and then he was standing right in front of the *mann* himself. The mask was daunting and made you think that death itself had come to this land. I couldn't help, but to admire Mitchell for his bravery. Mitchell was doing something ill advised, but he was doing it for good cause and I had to give it up to him for that.

El Diablo stepped forward with his gun taking out of a holster made of black leather. We could see everything as clear as day because the Moon was shining from above. I think I stopped breathing and my heart became still as ice. I watched as El Diablo moved that gun slowly up along the torso of Mitchell. He was trying to intimidate him, make him feel fear, but all he got was a stoic Mitchell looking back. I couldn't see his face, but I was reasonably sure that he wasn't given him the satisfaction of quivering in his boots.

When the gun came up to his head, I put my hand up to my mouth and wondered if the resounding crack of the gun going off would be the end of this rebellion.

I wanted to scream, cry and even run from this vehicle and down to protect him with my body. I was under the mistaken impression that a woman shielding him from danger would stop El Diablo from shooting the both of us. All we could do was watch and wait and hope to the *Gott* above that his time on this planet was not as short as it was seemed to be.

Chapter 3

I went for the door in a half baked attempt to help, but Jacob was right there to reel me back in. I look towards him and he was quite stern on this matter. We had been told by Mitchell to stay out of it and that he would handle things from here. I didn't like it and I didn't have to, but what I did have to do was give him room to breathe.

"We may not understand his way of life, but he has a way of seeing things from a different perspective. Bethany, we just need to give this time and hope that the next body that we have to carry out of here isn't his." That was a morbid thought and it brought to mind the makeshift grave that had been made for the many that had died during the catastrophe in Haiti. I remembered it and I didn't like it and it gave me nightmares for the first two weeks that I was here. The devastation was almost too much for me to bear.

I lay my head against Jacob's chest, still looking out at Mitchell and the way that he was taking the bull by the horns. He was through fighting in the shadows. It shocked me to learn that this was all his plan. He wanted El Diablo to find us. He had put out feelers to let El Diablo know that we were driving in this caravan of his own vehicles. I still couldn't believe that he said that to me. I was still trying to grasp onto the concept that he had everything well in hand.

It's usually me and Jacob that are the voice of reason. This time, he didn't even consult us, before he put this into motion.

"I guess I'm just used to being the leader. We were the ones that everybody turned to when they wanted help in the camp. We took that as a compliment and also the burden of responsibility that was given to us. I suppose Mitchell had the same thing happen to him and we're just going to have to trust that he knows what he's doing."

Suddenly, the forest lit up with other vehicles on either side of the road. People stormed out from behind the trees and we were now outnumbering El Diablo's men by too many to count.

"I do believe that this is where it's all going to go down. I know you want to go out there and join in on the fight, Jacob. I beg you on everything that is dear in our life that you don't do that. You're already finished telling me that I couldn't go, so I am making my plea to you to do the same thing." I could see that he was itching to go and his muscles were straining and he looked ready to burst at any second.

"It's hurting me to do nothing and I kind of like putting my hands on someone. It gave me a sense of doing something. I hate standing on the sidelines and waiting for everything to work out." I rolled down the window, pressing on the mechanism for the electric windows to go down. I never would understand all of these modern conveniences. It seemed like a lazy *mann's* way of going through life. I saw a simpler time here in Haiti. It reminded me of my own Amish community and how we all stuck together through hard times and the good times. Hard *Schaffe* was not something that we took lightly and we found ourselves enjoying putting our bodies to the test each and every day.

186

"What's the meaning of this, Mitchell? You know that I can just shoot you in the head and let you slump to the ground with your own blood pooling underneath you."

"I know that, EL Diablo. However, if you were to do that, you would make me a martyr and somebody else would pick up the mantle of leadership and run with it. Nobody has to die here today."

"I'm afraid that you're wrong about that, Mitchell." I saw him cock the gun with a smile that you could almost sense underneath the mask. Mitchell's hand came up and there was no explosion that followed from the lead leaving the chamber. There's just this calm feeling all around. Somehow, Mitchell had protected himself. It was making me feel like he was some kind of *Gott* amongst men.

"I don't know how he did that, but the gun was going to go off and it didn't. Do we take that as some sort of divine intervention on his behalf?" I really didn't know how to answer Jacob. I did make a silent prayer to the *mann* above. I even crossed my chest with two fingers and waited to see if Mitchell was going to be standing or dragged out of there as a corpse.

Suddenly, there was gunfire, but it wasn't coming from either Mitchell or El Diablo. They were now staring each other down with Mitchell holding onto the gun in some way to prevent it from going off. These men were from communities in the area that had been recruited to join up in this cause of peace. Once they realized that they weren't alone, they were willing to back up and become part of the solution.

I sensed Nicholas behind me. I looked back to see that he was holding onto his doctor's bag. He was ready to rush out there and do something to help those that were wounded or dying. It really did look like an old west showdown and people were falling with anguished cries. Mitchell and El Diablo stood in the middle of it unscathed and untouched by the bullets that were flying all around.

Chapter 4

It was very strange seeing these men fight to the death and the way that Mitchell and El Diablo seemed to be above it all. They were not talking anymore. They had come to an impasse. It felt like something was going to change and then just like that Nicholas was grabbing for the door.

"I don't think that you're going to go anywhere, Nicholas." I saw Jacob trying to prevent him from doing his duty as a *mann* of healing. "We're just going to get in the way and we need to wait until the smoke clears."

"I think that either you take your hands off me, Jacob, or I will make you take your hands off me. I'm not going to sit idly by and do nothing while people are hurting and dying. I need to be out there, whether it is putting me into the line of fire or not. You have to understand and I won't just let you stop me from playing God. Most doctors have a God complex and I'm not above that. I don't want to die, but I don't want anybody else to either.

Trust that God has a plan for all of us and that if it is my time, then I will walk into those bright lights with a smile on my face." I was quite impressed by his moxie. He wasn't afraid. He was putting his fear aside for the good of humanity

"Jacob, we can't in good conscience keep him here. His skills are not doing anybody any good. Gabrielle is in no immediate danger and he can do more out there than he can here. I think that he has the right idea and that we should join him." Jacob was trying to think of anything to say that would change my mind. I think he saw in my face that there was no way that I was going to.

"Fine, but stay down and keep your heads low. I have a bit of knowledge with first aid kits, so I can at least take care of those that are not too bad off. If I find something that I can't look after myself, I will call for you, Nicholas. In the meantime, I think that Nicholas and you should go out there and do what you can."

"I don't have to tell you that it's going to be dangerous, but don't expect me to try to stop you from helping. Jacob, I'll take Bethany with me to care for those that need immediate attention. She'll be my nurse and I'll use her to make sure that everybody is bandaged or given certain medications to ward off infection." As we were talking, the bullets were still ringing out in the night. They seemed to be slowing down slightly.

Some of Mitchell's men were taking shelter behind a couple of trees and firing at one of the vehicles of El Diablo's. There was return fire and neither one was going to back down.

We all took a deep breath and pulled the door open and raced out to render aid to those that needed it the most. I walked out and in my peripheral vision I could see that Jacob was doing exactly what he told us to do. He was keeping low and using the first aid kit that was given to him by Nicholas.

We were dealing with a sucking chest wound of one of El Diablo's men. It didn't matter to Nicholas and if it was enemy or friend, as long as it was bleeding and in need of care, it was going to get it. The *mann* was struggling to try to pull away from our help. He was already injured enough that there wasn't a whole lot of fight left in him.

"I think that you're going to need to hold him down. This is going to hurt like a mother." It was a strange saying, but I understood what he was trying to get at. I held the shoulders down and watched as he writhed in pain and agony over the wound that he had taken. "I'm going to pour some alcohol into this wound and he is going to thrash like you wouldn't believe." I wasn't sure if I knew what he meant, until he did what he said he was going to do. "

"Jesus, he's like a bucking bronco. I can't hold him down for too much longer." He was already stitching the wound and putting a pad over top of it to absorb some of the blood and hopefully make it come to a stop.

"You don't have to and we can't stay here and hold his hand. He's going to need some time to heal and as long as he doesn't put too much pressure on himself, he should be okay. We moved on to another one. I watched, as he opened this *mann's* shoulder to dig out the bullet that had lodged within. It was kind of fascinating to see the inside of a human body. You'd think that I would be squeamish or want to turn the other way. I wanted

192

to see this. It's not every day that you get to look in on *Gott's* creation.

"Bethany, you would make a great triage nurse in any emergency room. Where others would be throwing up into sinks, you would be standing there waiting for instructions. You have a real knack for healing and you have a bedside manner that makes other doctors look like they are only in it for the money." It was high praise coming from Nicholas a *mann* that had the necessary skills to dedicate to helping others. We were both of the same mind. I guess I did take solace in the fact that he was all about helping and not injuring.

"I'm going to need you to come over here, Nicholas." Jacob looked like he was out of his league. We raced over to see that this man had been riddled by at least five bullets. None of them hit his head. He had that going for him. Nicholas went right to work, ripping open his shirt and getting at the worst of the wounds first. It was amazing to see him work and under pressure and all that.

I could feel this shift in the air, something ominous shadowing what he was doing. He stopped with his hands on his chest after beating the living daylights out of him. His head was bowed and he looked up and shook his head. There was no life in this *mann's* eyes. He had jerked for a moment, but then he settled down with the death knell coming out of his mouth.

"There's nothing that I can do. I did everything I could, but it wasn't enough. It wasn't enough... It wasn't enough." This loss was affecting him and I put my hand over his shoulders to feel him shudder underneath my touch. He was crying and then he wiped those tears away walked. He went over to the next victim that needed his help. This guy was riddled with anxiety and guilt and yet he was still able to do his job. He was compartmentalizing his emotions.

I saw El Diablo use the distraction of what was going on around him to drop the gun and run into the forest with Mitchell hot on his tail. I couldn't let him do the same thing that he head done to Gabrielle's *bruder*. For the life of me, I couldn't remember his name and I think it started with a C. I felt so bad that I would forget something like that.

"Don't do it, Bethany." I could hear Jacob screaming my name. He was trying to prevent me from interfering, but it was to no avail. I was going to have my say, whether Mitchell wanted me to or not. I followed his trail through the broken branches. It wasn't that difficult with somebody with my hunting training. My *daett* had shown me everything that I needed to know. I was using those skills to track both men to where they were going to be.

Chapter 5

I felt the branches slapping against my arms and face and the stinging sensation was almost enough to make me stop my pursuit. I wasn't going to do that, because I knew that Mitchell had a one track mind. He had already told us that El Diablo had to be dealt with in the harshest terms. I didn't like the sound of that. I didn't question it at the time. If I was thinking right, I wouldn't even bother to get into the middle of this with these two men. They obviously had some unfinished business to settle between the two of them. I wasn't even sure that it was my place to do anything or say anything that would stop what was inevitably going to happen.

I did see the look in Mitchell's eyes, as he chased after him. If looks could kill, then El Diablo would have died from a heart attack at Mitchell's feet. If that were to happen, I could take it as a sign that it was supposed to. This was going to be in cold blood and I wasn't sure if Mitchell could come back from something like that.

"You don't know what you're doing, Mitchell. What you see isn't the true story and you need to listen to…AHHHHH." I heard the resounding snap of the gun cracking against El Diablo's jaw. I was still a little ways away, but I was on the right track.

"If you say one more word, then I'm going to kill you and I'll make you watch as I do it." I came into the clearing and he was standing over El Diablo with him on his knees waiting for an execution style death. "I don't want to hear anything more. You've already said your peace. If I were you, I would make a short prayer to your maker. Maybe he'll be more understanding about what you've done to the people of this land. I won't be; I've seen the devastation that you have caused and the way that you have capitalized on the misfortune of others. It sickens me and makes me even sicker to think that you made me into the man that I am today. I'm capable of killing in cold blood, because it's the only way."

The mask had been pulled off. I saw in this man's eyes a terror from the very idea that his life was soon to be over. This was not the same confident character that had been betraying everybody across this land. He was not conceited, arrogant or even putting up any sort of fight. It looked like he was a shell of the *mann* that he was before. I saw something, but I wasn't sure what it was. Something was nagging at me and was almost like the hairs in the back of my neck had risen to warn me that there was something seriously off about all of this.

I really didn't have time to delve into that, because I had to stop Mitchell from doing something that would change the way that he looked at himself in the mirror. If he did this, then the person that he looked at in the mirror would be a killer and not just somebody that did it because it was in self defense or a moment of complete madness.

"Don't do it, Mitchell and he's not worth it."

"Listen to her...for God's sake listen to her." He was begging for his life, crying of all things. He didn't look like any sort of threat to me.

"You've broken him and you can drag him back to show the others that he is not as scary as they once thought. He's in the same position that he put Jacob in with a gun up against his forehead. He doesn't look into the face of death and laugh at it. He cries and he's just a bully that needed somebody to come around and show him that his actions have consequences." I was saying anything I could to try to get Mitchell's attention. He was circling El Diablo with his gun drawn and ready to use it at a moment's notice.

"I...I...don't want to...die. I have...two kids and a wife waiting for me at home in Texas. I'm not who you think I am."

"No, you are not and without your mask, you're nothing. You should be ashamed of yourself. You now know that my people are not going to take it anymore."

"I'll leave and never look back. Just let me live... Please... I want to live." There was something wrong here. I got the sense that El Diablo was hiding behind that mask in a different sense. This was something that had to be looked into, but I couldn't do that with El Diablo dead.

"I know that it gives you a unique thrill to see him like this, Mitchell. He has wrecked havoc against your people and made them think that he would kill them if they didn't comply with his wishes and demands. You need to look into his eyes and see what I'm seeing." He didn't even appear to be looking at me. I think he was trying his best to drown me out. He needed to do that. If he didn't, then I would get under his skin. He wasn't going to allow that to happen.

"I really don't have to do anything, Bethany. I really wish that you didn't come here. I'm afraid that you going to see something that is going to take you by complete shock." I wanted to say something to convince him that there was a better way. I thought that I could do that, because I already pulled him back from the brink a couple of times.

"I don't want to…" It was El Diablo's last words. Mitchell stood as still as he could and fired that weapon point blank into the back of El Diablo's head. He looked at me and I looked at him. We both knew that he was never going to survive a mortal wound like that one. He fell forward with the help of Mitchell's boot kicking him in the back of the head. Mitchell dragged him by the collar and tossed him over the edge of the cliff and down to the rocks below. He had done it and I knew that he was going to, but to see it was another matter altogether

I saw evil for the first time and it didn't come at the hands of El Diablo. I saw that same evil glinting in Mitchell's eyes. I could not reach him. He wouldn't let me. This was like a building had collapsed on me with no escape. I was completely speechless.

Chapter 6

I think that I was in a state of shock at what I had seen. I replayed it over and over again in my head and looked for any way that I could possibly prevent it. I had pleaded with Mitchell to keep this *mann* alive as a symbol to the others that might try the same thing. His public trial would make anybody see him, as the coward that he was. I thought that I was getting through to him. I was foolish to think that he was going to change his mind.

His hand was not even shaking, but I saw this look in his eyes that told me that he didn't enjoy that in the very least. It didn't matter. He had changed in my eyes. I couldn't look at him the same way ever again. Cold-blooded murder was something that I could not condone and would not give him forgiveness for. It was the first time that I didn't think that I could save him. It made me feel like I was useless.

He stayed there looking out over the cliff and down at the body below. He was splayed out on the rocks in an awkward angle. I began to hit Mitchell against his stomach with my tiny little fists flying in rage. I haven't hit anybody in my life, but this was something that was too hard for me to control. He didn't even flinch. He let me wail on him, until I finally fell on to my knees weeping like a little girl.

If he was any sort of man, he would've been there with me, but he stood there as stoic as ever. He was not smiling or showing any kind of emotion. It was only in his eyes that I saw regret, but maybe that was just my idea of wishful thinking.

"Bethany, he had to go and from the moment I began this campaign of peace, I knew that this was going to be the outcome. I just didn't have the courage to tell you. I don't think that you would've followed me. I'm afraid that I kept it from you for selfish reasons. I wanted you around. I needed your wise counsel and strong convictions to keep me from losing myself. There was a part that hoped that you would get through to me and that I would let this man live and face persecution by everybody that he had made suffer. Unfortunately, that part of me that showed kindness to others was only brief. I still had a blood lust in my heart. He had to die and I'm sorry you had to see that, but I beg you for forgiveness." He was running his hands through my hair and I looked up at him to see that there was a lone tear in his eye.

I stood on shaky legs and faced him. "I know you want me to give you some kind of absolution, but there's no way that I can. I can't even look at you. It hurts me to say this, but I don't think I even want to talk to you." I turned to walk away, but his hands gripped my shoulders very tightly to prevent me from taking even one step.

"You don't understand. He couldn't be allowed to breathe the same air that we do. I didn't want to do it and I would rather be working on my charcoal drawings than to be put into position of judge jury and executioner. I know you don't like what I did, but I need you to be here for me. Without you, I don't know if I can survive. Mentally speaking, I'm hanging by a thread and you have no idea how much I'm grasping onto you as my own personal life preserver. You're the only one that can help me and I know that I don't deserve it."

"NO, Mitchell, I can't give you what you want. I just don't have it in me. You've killed that part that wants to save you. I've done that already twice and I thought that I was making a difference, but you didn't even flinch when you fired that gun. Maybe if you had done it with shaky hands, I might have seen that you were hurting, but you didn't." I wrenched away from his hands. I was walking away, while at the same time hearing his footsteps following from behind. He wasn't chasing me and I didn't even give him the respect of turning and seeing his pain in his eyes.

I'd done what I could to give him a fighting chance, but he was already lost and he was going to have to find himself. I couldn't do that for him, not after what I had seen him do with his own two hands. The image of that gun going off and the way that he was so cold about it made me wonder if I even had a chance to save him in the first place.

As we came out of the clearing, everybody had gathered together, including Jacob and Nicholas.

They waited and I walked over to Jacob and curled myself underneath his arm and against his chest. He held me lovingly and I think he knew that I had seen something that had severely affected me.

It wasn't long before Mitchell came out with the smoking barrel of his gun leading the way. He looked around with this cold calculating stare. He then raised the gun in triumph. "He's dead. There is no more El Diablo." He watched as everybody cheered and screamed praises of Glory in his name. I could see that he would never be the same again and death would follow him like a dark cloud over his head. Even Nicholas shook his head, like he couldn't believe that it was over. Maybe it had more to do with the fact that another human being had lost their life. My Amish background made me want to help, but I just couldn't bring myself to move away from the comforting arms of my beloved.

"It's going to be OK Bethany… It's going to be OK." I knew that Jacob was only trying to soothe away my worries. I don't think anything could wipe away the image of Mitchell gunning down a *mann* with no way to defend himself.

Chapter 7

"I know that this is bothering you, Bethany and maybe if you say it out loud it won't have that kind of hold on you." It had been a day since I had seen Mitchell turn into a cold-blooded killer that he had claimed to be all along. I'd tried to sleep, only to find myself seeing El Diablo face and the terrified expression that came from knowing that his life was over. He could only stare as a bullet entered into his brain and never came out. He opened his mouth in surprise at feeling his life begin to drain from his body.

"I don't even want to tell you how horrifying the sight of him killing El Diablo was. I hope to *Gott* that you never have to witness something like that yourself. I saw the same look in his eyes that he had when he put the gun to your head. He had placed you on the ground ready to sacrifice you. No, I can't say that it was the same look. At least when he had the gun to your head, there seemed to be something inside of him struggling to do it or not to do it."

"I'm not sure what you're trying to tell me, Bethany." I didn't want to say what was on my mind, but he was pushing me and there was just so much that I could take.

"He had no heart, no compassion and there was this coldness that surrounded him like a shroud of death itself. He was that *mann's* judge jury and executioner and he felt no remorse for what he did. I saw in his eyes that he thought that it was the right thing to do. Did I tell you that El Diablo begged for his life and for the life of his kids and wife?"

"No...No... you didn't say any of that. I guess I wouldn't want to be in your shoes. I think that I can see and feel the pain that's coming off of you. You've been through a lot and I know that you and Mitchell will never be friends again. I just hope that we can put this ugliness behind us and concentrate on the good work that we've been doing. It's probably best that we leave him to his campaign of peace and return to the camp. I know that you don't want to stay here any longer than you have to."

We'd made our way back to his hometown and people were treating him like he was a hero. To me, he was a coward and I don't think that I could've made others see it from my point of view. He had killed without emotion and that made him some kind of psychopath in my mind. They gave him a hero's welcome with a feast fit for a king. He was treated like royalty from the moment that he arrived back in town. He told them that he was not through and that peace was a never ending struggle. They needed to stay vigilant at all times. I did admire the fact that he was still willing to fight the good fight against any enemy that decided to fill the vacuum that was left after El Diablo was taken out.

"I do want to leave; Jacob and I don't want to see Mitchell's face or that smug smile ever again. He has caused me to rethink what it is to be a good person. I thought that he was one, but he proved me wrong. I won't be fooled again." When I saw that *mann* die right in front of me, I felt a little piece of myself had died right alongside him. He wasn't even given the dignity of a funeral. He was left there for whatever wildlife to find him and pick the carcass apart.

"For now, we are going to have to pretend. I will make arrangements for us to leave here shortly. Just try to keep quiet. I know how that's going to be hard and that you obviously have something to say to Mitchell. He may be basking in a false hero worship, but these people need that hero. We can't take that away from them. He gave them back their lives. They may no longer have to worry about soldiers coming to their village to take something that isn't theirs."

"I know they need this, but it galls me to know that he could stand there and take the adulation without something nagging at his conscience. He should reveal to them just what kind of monster he has become." I want to slap him across his face for being a hypocrite. Mitchell needed somebody to bring him down off his pedestal. If people continued to treat him as a hero, he would start to think that what he did was right. He would start to think that there was no justice and that the only justice came at the hands of a gun and violence.

He was not a *mann* to be cheered. I would not stand by and let him think that his actions didn't have any consequences. Then again, I'm not even sure that I wanted to speak to him, let alone see him at all. It might be better that I just walk away and try to help people that could be helped. I was wasting my time on a *mann* that obviously only wanted to use me to wipe his consciousness clean.

Chapter 8

"Remember, we are happy for all of them. We are now going to return to what we do best. We can't show any cracks and believe me, I feel same way that you do. You probably feel it more deeply than I. I wasn't there to witness the atrocity that he had committed." He was right and had he seen what I'd seen, he wouldn't be trying to put up a good face in front of others.

Mitchell was sitting in one of the pews in the church that had been built recently by the community. How he was able to sit there and not burst into flames for what he had done was beyond me. He was supported by his inner circle. Nicholas and Patrick were right by his side. I didn't see how Nicholas could be here at all, but apparently he was willing to wash his hands in dirty water like the rest of them.

"We've gathered here today to tell you that we're going back to our camp. We've done everything we can for all of you. With El Diablo gone we can concentrate on what we do best. We still have a lot of houses to build for those that don't have roofs over their heads. We know that you'll understand and we hope to *Gott* that you are all able to find your way in relative peace and harmony." I could see that he was directing his comments or at least the last portion of it towards Mitchell.

At least Mitchell looked like he was uneasy. He shifted nervously in his seat. He had not tried to defend what he had done. The only person that he showed any remorse or regret for putting a bullet in that *mann's* head was to me. He wanted my forgiveness and I could not give him what I didn't feel. The minister of this church was sitting beside. I had a feeling that Mitchell was not exactly upfront about what he did, not even to his minister. I think that he was going to take the fact that in that moment he enjoyed killing that man to his grave.

"I don't know about everybody else, but I'm going to miss you. You showed remarkable resolve in the face of overwhelming odds. You never wavered and you even walked into a line of fire to help those of the enemy. I still think that you could be a good nurse or even a Dr., Bethany." It was nice of him to say that, but Nicholas really couldn't wrap his mind around the Amish lifestyle. We did not believe in modern medicine and for the most part we used homemade remedies and herbs to cure what ails us. It was only after those measures had been taken that didn't work that we turned to other forms of medical help.

"I only did what I thought was right and from the moment that I came here it was always been my intention to leave you better than what you were. We may have not come here on own free will, but we are glad that we did. I'm afraid that the scars of what we did during this expedition of peace will forever change each and every one of us. Things that we've seen will haunt us and make us wake up in a cold sweat in the morning. It's all part of living and I just hope that everybody can live with what they've done in the name of peace." I didn't mean it, but I was getting a little serious. People were looking at me like they weren't sure what I was trying to get at.

"My wife just wants everybody to be happy and we know that we have done everything we can here. Others need our help and I'm afraid that means that we're going to have to take our leave. We appreciate the hospitality and if we are back around this way anytime soon, we'll be sure to stop by and see how everything is going."

Jacob was now trying to smooth the waters. I had ruffled some feathers and made them look at me like I was out of my mind. This was the time to stand united and even though I didn't feel much like celebrating, I tried to put on enough of a face to fake it.

Everybody congratulated us and told us that without us none of this could happen. That gave me a shiver and Goosebumps began to appear on my skin. I think that Jacob knew what I was feeling. He had kept me close the entire time that he had made his speech. We had gone over each word and what I had said was very much improvised. There was no denying that I wanted nothing to do with Mitchell for what he did, but I was glad that they found the peace that they were looking for.

We walked out of there and over to the bus that they had taken from us at the start of all this. I was about to climb inside, when I felt a hand on my shoulder and turned to see Mitchell. He looked like he had something to say, but I wasn't sure that I wanted to hear anything from him.

"I know that you don't understand, but it had to be done. I'm not trying to convince you that what I did was right, because I don't think that I could even if I tried. I just want you to know that I feel bad about it. It's something that I'm going to have to live with for the rest my life. Nobody else will know what I felt during that time, except for maybe you, Bethany. That is something that we will share between us." I nodded my head solemnly, gave him a brief hug, nothing that would show him that I was on board with any of this.

I turned and walked into the bus and went back to where my husband was now waiting for me. I sat down and he held my hand and then we looked out and watched as the people waved and gave us a sendoff that brought a tear to my eye metaphorically speaking. I couldn't look at Mitchell and I saw him turn and walk through the crowd without saying a word. His soul was now tainted and would forever be so, until the day he finally walked up to the pearly gates and looked to *Gott* to judge him for his actions.

Chapter 9

"Bethany, you have to know that he's a good *mann* deep down. He wanted the best for his family and for his people. The way he went about it was maybe not the right way, but it was the only way that he knew to take care of things." Jacob was trying to plead Mitchell's case. I don't think he really agreed with his methods, but he didn't want me to think that we had failed Mitchell. "You have to admit that we did show him another way. It's up to him if he's going to follow it or not. I think we both know that he has in the past. I think we can take a bit of comfort from knowing that we've given him a conscience."

"I'm not sure that we did, but if we did, then maybe he will think twice before he does something like that again. It stands to reason that he would be a different *mann* if it wasn't for us. I don't think that there was anything that we could do to change what he was going to do to El Diablo, when he finally got his hands on him. That was already stuck in his head. I feel guilty for not doing enough." We were sitting on the bus and the kids were by themselves in the back. I turned to see that they were talking very low. They didn't want somebody to hear what they were saying. Frankie looked back at me for a moment and his expression changed to one of gratitude.

"Bethany, I'm not condoning what he did, but I don't think anybody could have stopped him. You can't lay this on your shoulders. It wasn't your fault that he fired the gun. That was his decision. He could've made a different one, but he didn't. Don't feel guilty. His mind was already set from the moment that he heard that El Diablo was hurting the people that he loved the most. I don't know what I would have done in his shoes, but I would hope that I would learn that violence was never the answer."

"You're right and violence is not the answer, Jacob. We both know that violence usually leads to more violence. There has to be an end to the cycle of death. If not, then something else will visit Mitchell; he has already turned the pages of his future by killing El Diablo. Whatever path he chooses will be soaked in that blood and he will have to walk through it to get to the other side." Mitchell would never forget the moment that that gun went off and I hope that each and every night that he would hear that *mann* pleading for his life.

"Put it behind you, Bethany and move on to something more pleasurable. Our camp is not too far away and we will be there momentarily." I did look forward to going back to the camp. I glanced towards Gabrielle to see that she was still very quiet. It made me feel like she was hiding something, or maybe she was just grieving for her *bruder*. She didn't seem to condemn us or hold us responsible, but there was something going on behind her eyes.

I tried to reach out to her several times but she always rebuffed my friendship. She told me that she needed time to deal with everything, but she was glad that I was taking her back to our camp. I told her everything about it and she listened intently, until finally I had nothing else to say. She said that she was going to enjoy meeting the people that came here to make a difference.

220

I would have to have a talk with the kids, because they were entering a new chapter of their lives. I didn't want them to be scared or think that I wasn't going to be with them every step of the way. Frankie would stay with me and Jacob. We had decided together that we would look after him and give him the life that he deserved. I wanted to show him that death did not have to follow him wherever he went. That devastation did not have to mean the end of everything that he held close to his heart.

"Jacob, I'm glad that you wanted to do what's right for the *kinner* and Frankie. He was just looking out for his friends and we can't fault him for wanting to protect them from harm. It's going to be interesting to put a hammer in his hands and see how he deals with manual labor." My intention was to find him a home, but I secretly found myself wanting to bring him back to my *dochtah*, as a surrogate big *bruder*.

Chapter 10

I was hopeful for the future and if I could stop thinking about Mitchell long enough to help others, then maybe I could wash my hands of what he did. I still felt like I was partly responsible. I replayed the incident and tried to come up with something that I could say that would've made a difference. There didn't seem to be anything. I suddenly realized that Mitchell had almost pulled me into the quicksand with him. I was able to pull free, but he was still sinking ever deeper with each breath that he took. Hopefully he would find somebody to pull him free, but it wasn't going to be me.

Gabrielle walked up to the front of the bus and sat down with her hands on the railing. Mitchell's man Patrick had come along to give us a hand. We didn't need anybody else's help. We didn't want to appear rude, so we took Mitchell's man Patrick. Maybe he would stay around long enough to see all the good work that we had been doing in this land.

"Jacob, we came here to help and then we were pulled into a fight that really wasn't ours. We should have walked away, but I knew that neither one of us could do that in good conscience. We are good religious folk and we would never turn down somebody's plea for help. I wonder what going to happen to Mitchell." There was a part of me that wanted him to find a way to live with what he did, but there was also another part that hoped that he would suffer for his misdeeds. These were two different parts of my soul battling for supremacy and I had no idea which one was going to win out in the end. I had to believe that I would want nothing but the best for Mitchell, but right now I had condemned him to his own personal hell.

"He'll find his way. we all do with the help of others." Jacob looked ready to roll up his sleeves and get back to *schaffe*. I was right there along with him. We finally came into camp and everybody became, so quiet that the only thing you could hear was the crackling of the fire.

We walked off the bus in a trance. We both walked over to the Deacon who was standing there and looking at the ashes. We put our hands in between his and we stood there and looked at the burned wreckage of the homes that we had put together.

All of them had been rendered down to ashes and there was the symbol of El Diablo burned into the surface of the wood. I thought that we were done with this and then I turned to see that the *kinner* were now muttering something underneath their breath. I followed their eyes and saw that there was no sign of Gabrielle. She was gone and I turned and knew that this was not the end, but a deadly beginning. We would rebuild. Whoever had taken on the guise of El Diablo would not get away with it.

"I don't understand how any of this can happen. We're only trying to help. Who would do such a thing?" I could see the confusion in the Deacon's eyes and all I could do was hold his hand. Jacob did the same thing to the other. We weren't going home and we still had a lot to do. All of our good work had apparently been for nothing.

Rachel H. Kester

END OF THIS BOXSET...

But you will probably love the next book!

>>> Click Here if you want to read the next
Episode before everyone <<<

17603775R00126

Made in the USA
Middletown, DE
27 November 2018